Indians discovered a massacred wagon train. The lone survivor was a naked white youth crying for his dead mother and father.

A locket in the boy's hand, when opened, revealed his name and age — Ned Ladigo, three years old.

Ladigo was accepted as a member of the tribe, and years later he and Running Deer were joined in a tribal marriage that brutally ended when she was murdered. "I must be with her. I must . . . I cannot live without her." His hand reached for his knife . . .

This book is a work of fiction. Names, characters, places, and incidents either are products of the author's imagination or are used fictitiously. Any resemblance to actual events or locales or persons, living or dead, is entirely coincidental.

Love is Forever
Copyright © 2020 Wayne Greenough
ISBN: 978-1-4874-3046-7
Cover art by Martine Jardin

Published by eXtasy Books Inc or
Devine Destinies, an imprint of eXtasy Books Inc

Look for us online at:
www.eXtasybooks.com or www.devinedestinies.com

Love is Forever

By

Wayne Greenough

DEDICATION

This story is dedicated to my dear wife, June Greenough

CHAPTER ONE

Ned Ladigo snuggled Running Deer to his chest to hear her heartbeat. It pounded erratically, struggled gallantly in its dying effort to find its normal rhythm, failing, failing. *No . . . She mustn't die. She mustn't.* A scream dashing from his throat was heard by the tribe. "Running Deer, you're my life, my forever love. You must not leave me."

Blood spurted from her mouth when she coughed. She struggled to talk. Her voice came to him as a whisper. "I love you Ned, Ladigo. I will always love you. Hold me. Hold me tight, my forever love."

Running Deer sighed once before she died. Ladigo felt her life leave her body.

No. Please no

Tears flowed from his eyes. They fell upon Running Deer's and slowly closed their glittering blackness. He held her in his arms.

"I shall hold you forever, my Running Deer. I shall never let you go. I will never leave you. Hear me Running Deer. I will never leave you." He kissed her lips. They were cold and lifeless.

An elderly woman of the tribe touched his arm. Through tear-soaked vision, Ladigo recognized her as Running Deer's grandmother. Now she was an all alone woman, now she was without her granddaughter, now she was without anyone. There were no tears in her dark eyes, only a deep grief he knew would remain forever, always in her eyes and facial expression.

1

"Running Deer is no longer with us in body, Ned Ladigo," she said in her always quiet voice. "She is now with us in spirit, where she shall always be for all eternity. You must put her remains aside."

"I cannot. I must hold her forever."

"You shall hold her forever in your heart. But now you must let her body go. You must."

Ladigo stood with Running Deer wrapped in his arms. He took three steps and stooped to gently place her among the soft pile of buffalo skins in the wigwam's corner. He kissed her cold lips, touched her face, before turning to her killer.

Buffalo Man, a jealous lover, stared at Running Deer, blood dripping from his knife. He threw the weapon from him. It landed at Ladigo's feet. Buffalo Man's love for Running Deer had never been accepted by her.

"I cannot love you," she had always said to him. She had even laughed at his proposal. "I never shall."

"Why, Buffalo Man? Why?" Words choked in Ladigo's throat, stopping him from saying more. Instead he grabbed the deer antler handle of his Bowie Knife, felt the cold deadliness of its steel blade. He would kill Buffalo Man and then he would take his own life. Without Running Deer there was no need for him to remain alive.

Before he could plunge his knife into Buffalo Man's heart, the man collapsed to his knees. His ugly face became a deadly sneer, as if a blazing hot fire raged throughout his body. He gave Ladigo a twisted smile of triumph when he spoke. "Stay your hand, Ned Ladigo. I have done my death for you. I have consumed a solution of hemlock from the silver cup that I now bequeath to you . . . I have cursed the cup . . . Should you drink from it you also shall die . . . I doubt that you will ever put the cup to your lips, for you are destined to live a full life . . . I have slain Running Deer so that in life you may never have her . . . I shall have her . . . I join her in death. You . . .

you, Ned Ladigo . . . will forever suffer from the terrible agony of loneliness, knowing that Running Deer is with me . . . and she will be mine. My spirit and her spirit will join . . . she shall be mine . . . mine . . . forever."

Buffalo Man died. In death, his twisted sneer remained.

A fury raged through Ned Ladigo. Barely aware of what he was doing, he stabbed his long knife again and again into Buffalo Man's dead heart, until he felt his knife hand being stayed by someone's steel-hard muscled fingers. He then slumped to the ground and sobbed.

CHAPTER TWO

Three years before Running Deer's murder, a petty criminal named Michael was frantically running from seven vigilantes who unanimously agreed that Michael was to be fitted for a proper size to their new hemp necktie. Michael's crimes weren't big, no stagecoaches, no banks, no trains. He specialized in easy thefts, such as stealing from mercantile stores and churches, which quite often would leave small amounts of coin money in unlocked desk drawers. It was easy pickings for him and certainly worth a chuckle and a long night of boozing with the willing dance hall ladies. But his luck had gone bad the night he robbed a church. He was caught by seven drunken vigilantes, and all he had managed to filch was a bible.

Michael had escaped the rope by running his horse to death and then using his feet until he dropped from exhaustion, face down with his nose in the dirt.

The Nanesko Tribe that housed Ned Ladigo had found him, protected him, and became certain he was a Sky Pilot, a genuine bible thumper, one who was never without the bible grasped in his left hand.

Because of the bible, the Nanesko had assumed Michael was a man of the cloth. They protected him from the hemp necktie, and Michael played the role of a preacher to the hilt. It was like acting in a melodrama, and all he had to do was read a few sentences from the bible. He spoke many religious words to the tribe. Some listened to his Sunday Sermons while others laughed at them. He taught the white man's language to Ned Ladigo and Running Deer.

After the tribe's chief performed the tribal marriage, there were many smiles of pure joy. Ned and Running Deer, a perfect couple, were joined for many happy years together.

But then Buffalo Man's madness changed everything. Now a great sorrow saturated the Indian village. Tears flowed from every face along with wailing moans of grief.

Michael touched Ladigo's shoulder. He had words from the bible which, if said properly in his soothing voice, would hopefully calm the young man down.

Shock coursed through the man of the cloth as he saw the devastating grief on the young man's face. Before he could speak his usual biblical paragraphs, words of grief were being shouted at him.

"Go say your words of nonsensical wisdom to those who will listen. Unless you can perform a miracle that brings Running Deer back to me alive and well, I do not wish to see you or hear your sympathetic nothing words that you will read to me from that worthless book you never fail to have tucked away under your left arm or in your hands."

Michael nodded and shrugged his shoulders. He walked away to join people who would listen to his words.

Chapter Three

Five days were to pass before Running Deer's burial ritual was completed. People from the Indian Village flocked around Ned Ladigo. They said words of farewell. They knew he was leaving the tribe. He barely heard their words. The numbness and shock of Running Deer's death was wracking his soul. He did manage to nod when a young girl of some fourteen summers kissed his lips. Her name was Raven. She mumbled words of love to him as her tears fell on his leather shirt. Seconds later she turned and ran from him.

Ladigo managed a smile. There was nothing left for him here. He stuffed several days of food into leather pouches, along with his meager belongings and Buffalo Man's poisonous silver cup. In a hip sheath was his Bowie Knife, on his back was his quiver of arrows and a sturdy bow. He mounted the tribe's fastest horse and rode off without looking back. That way no one saw his tears. They did hear his screams echoing from the nearby mountains.

CHAPTER FOUR

Ladigo thought about ending his life. A few jabs with the Bowie knife in the heart area would end his life . . . Why not?

He grabbed the bone handle of his knife, pulled it from its sheath and touched his heart area with the knife's point. One shove into his chest, that was all it should take. *Go ahead, shove* . . . He shook all over. His body was rebelling, telling him no . . . no . . . that Running Deer would never want him to do such a terrible thing. He must live on . . . He threw his knife into the brush and urged his horse into a gallop.

A few days later Ladigo came across a wagon train of friendly people looking for what they called the Promised Land. To suppress his normally stoic outlook toward relationships with strangers, and suffering the loneliness of the trail, he joined the wagon train. The people were a happy lot, who taught him much more of the white man's language, especially their religious beliefs. They assured him that his murdered wife, Running Deer, waited for him in a place called Heaven. Buffalo Man, they adamantly declared, burned forever in a satanic place known as Hell.

Ned Ladigo tried to accept the white man's way of biblical thinking. But he found their bible full of doubts and lies, so he knew not what to believe. How often had he asked them if the white man's Heaven and the Indian's Spirit World were the same place? Sadly, no one could answer his question.

After several months he left the Wagon Train. The desire

to travel the next trail, to see if it would lead to the peace he so desired piqued his curiosity and overflowed. So off he went.

Weeks passed as Ladigo blazed the trails. He ate berries and the roots of plants he recognized. With his bow and arrows he shot small animals. One day he came across a group of people building a church. A man welcomed him, declared he was Father Eliza Jones and asked if he knew how to drive nails without bending them? He nodded, and was put to work.

The days flew by as he pounded away with a claw hammer driving shiny nails into cedar smelling shingles. The church would be completed soon.

But then trouble arrived. Men came on horses, men with guns.

CHAPTER FIVE

"Here they come," Ned heard Father Eliza Jones shout to his flock of people. His words rang with the sound of discouragement. "Remember, all of you, we are a peace-loving people who will not do any form of harm to man or beast."

Ladigo spat shingle nails from his mouth, fitted the claw hammer to the leather belt buckled around his waist, and slid down the ladder he'd hung on to while shingling the church roof. Landing feet first in the soft dirt, he walked to Father Jones.

"Tell me what is happening." he asked. "Why are we being invaded by a half dozen men on horses?"

There were tears in Father Jones' eyes. "They have come to burn down our church. They warned me they would do so."

"Burn down the church? Why would they do such a terrible act?"

"Because, Ned, they have deeds, deeds that declare, unbeknown to us, that we have built our church on their property. We cannot stop them from what they are about to do."

"Have you seen those deeds?" Ladigo asked.

"No, I have not. But they declared they have them."

Ladigo asked "I fail to understand . . . what is wrong with building a church?"

"Nothing is wrong . . . it is what my people have longed for. But the judge and his sheriff partner have declared otherwise. There is to be no church as long as they say so, and they are the law."

"Then, Father Jones, the law shall stop saying no to you. A

church you will have. I vow to you, a church you will have."

Father Jones shook his head. "Take a close look at them, Ned Ladigo. The men you see before you rule the town. Notice that the sheriff, the judge, and their four deputies all have holstered weapons strapped to their waists, guns that will be used against us if we raise our hands in defiance. And note the long poles with oil-soaked rags on them that each man carries. When lit and tossed into the church, their flames will destroy what we have worked so many days to accomplish."

Ladigo watched as a heavyset man with a bulbous nose, wiped sweat from his face before he hollered, "You know why we're here, Father Jones."

"And who might you be?" Ladigo asked.

The heavyset man's high-pitched laugh echoed. The men on horses snickered. One could be heard mumbling something about being a stupid dumb fool.

"I'm Judge Follett," the man yelled. "This church is on my property. I do not want a church. I'm here to see that it is burned down to the ground. Don't try to stop us. We have guns that we'll use against you."

"Why must the church be destroyed?" Ladigo asked, staring at him.

For a few seconds the judge's expression looked as if he didn't know what to say next. Ladigo saw this and stared intently at the man in an attempt to rattle him.

After glancing at the sheriff, who whispered something, the judge asked, "Who are you, young man?"

"I'm Ladigo, Ned Ladigo. I repeat my question. Why must this church be destroyed? If it's on your property, and you say it is, sell us the land the church is on." Ladigo turned to face Father Jones. "Have I said too much? Is there enough money saved to buy the land the church sets on?"

Father Jones nodded. "If Judge Follett will ask a fair price . . . yes, we will buy the land."

"No deal," shouted the judge at Father Jones' offer. "My land will never be sold to a bunch of simpering Bible Thumpers. The church will be burned down to the ground, and you and your people must leave my land. If any of you are seen anywhere on my property, even a single foot of it, in the next twenty-four hours, I'll have my men shoot them and you. You've been warned, all legal like, so get out. All right men, burn the church."

Ladigo shouted. "Wait. Do you have the papers that declare we're on your property with you? If so, I wish to see them."

Judge Follett wiped more sweat from his face before saying, "They are in my office safe. Not here."

Ladigo smiled. "Then I will come to see them."

Three of the deputies drew their guns. At that Ladigo merely shrugged his shoulders. "If you shoot me in front of all these people, how is that legal? I will come tonight, Judge, to see those papers. Have them ready for me."

Ladigo could not stop what the men came to do. They quickly lit their torches. One nodded at Ladigo and smiled.

CHAPTER SIX

It took a friendly discussion with Father Brown and his flock before they realized Ladigo was stubborn to the point of being inflexible. If he decided to do something, he would do it, no matter what.

Father Brown gave a long sigh before giving up. "Very well, Ned Ladigo, you have chosen to leave us. What you have in mind goes against all we believe in. I hope God will protect you."

Ladigo smiled and said, "God and the Great Spirit. They will do just that and perhaps even more."

It was still somewhat light out when Ladigo started his walk to the town, which was three miles away from the burned down church.

For what he planned to do, he needed the dark and he needed the town's mercantile owner, Zeke Ezekiel.

Daylight was rapidly fading away when Ladigo reached his destination. The mercantile's oaken entrance door was closed and no inside lamps were lit as he began making loud hammering noises on the battered wash tub hanging from the store's right-side wall on two rusty nails. It made a loud drumming noise, enough to waken Ezekiel and the dead on boot hill.

It took several minutes before he started hearing crabby shouts coming from inside the mercantile.

"Is that you again, Alky, you drunken old fool? Did you

get yourself booted out of the saloon like you did for more times than I can count, and now you want some of my whiskey? Is that it? Well, you won't get any, if that's what's on your soused-up-mind."

Ladigo heard Ezekiel's throat make a loud rasping sound like a saw striking a spike just before he shouted more words.

"All right, all right, stop that infernal racket before you wake up the dead. I'm coming. Hold your horses. Stop that stampeding noise. Don't bash in the door, you . . . you . . . worthless hunk of nothing. Damn and blast it, where's a candle, when I need one to see what I'm doing?"

A moment later Ezekiel swung the mercantile's outside door wide open. He gazed angrily at a figure all dressed in black clothing until a match was lit showing the man's face. "Why . . . sake's alive . . . Ned Ladigo . . . Heavens lad, whatever are you doing here at this hour? You're all alone. Is something wrong?"

"Yes, much is wrong," Ladigo said, "and I am here to correct it. I must ask a favor of you."

"Name it. For you I will grant it."

"I have need of a knife and a gun."

Ladigo heard Ezekiel gulp. He saw the man's surprised look just before the match burned itself out. In the darkness he heard the mercantile owner's words. "I must ask why. Those weapons are not to Father Jones' liking."

Ladigo answered. "That is true. But I am no longer under his guidance. I have left his following because of the terribly wrong things done to him and his people. A few hours earlier, his church was burned down to the ground. He and his followers were told to leave Judge Follett's property in twenty-four hours. If they failed to do so they would be shot on sight. That is why I have need for a gun and a knife. I cannot face the judge and the sheriff without them. They would shoot me."

Zeke Ezekiel snorted his disdain, "The judge, the sheriff, and that miserable gun slinging bunch of fools he pinned deputy badges on. For hours now I've heard them loudly shouting and bragging about their infamous deeds. They're out carousing and raising hell all over the town. My last customer told me they were also busy drinking the saloon dry. You think you can change all that? Do you?"

Ladigo nodded with certainty. "Yes, I feel that I can, I hope that I can. Before the burning of the church, the judge bragged aloud for all to hear. To me, the sound of his trembling voice and his words made me think that perhaps he is a cowardly person. The sneering faces of the sheriff and his four deputies and their alcoholic smell portrayed them as drunkards, and perhaps cowardly back shooters, except for one who somehow seemed somewhat different."

Zeke muttered. "That one man was likely Jake Larson. He's not a user of alcohol. But I've heard people say he's a downright mean gunslinger, lightning fast with a gun, and he's a man with no fear. If he's forced to kill a person, he makes certain it's a face-to-face shootout where the other man has a chance to outdraw him."

The mercantile man became silent. Finally, he sighed twice before whispering as if to himself, "If I help you, Ned, I'll be asking for trouble, and I sure will receive it. But then I've been gun whipped more than once in my life." Another sigh and silence. Then, "Oh tarnation, what of it? I reckon one more beating should give me just a few more scars along with lots more complaining. It will certainly increase my dislike for what has happened to this town. The judge is as crooked as any human can be. So are the sheriff and that mangy bunch of gun toting idiots he calls deputies. Come in out of the dark lad, find a chair. I'll stoke up the fire, put on coffee, and get what you asked for."

An hour passed. Ned Ladigo drank steaming hot coffee

and puffed away on his short stem pipe before the mercantile man reappeared. Ezekiel was breathing hard due to being loaded down with a gun belt full of bullets, a holstered gun, and a long-bladed-Bowie Knife. Ezekiel drew the gun from its holster and shoved it in his belted trousers. "How much do you know about guns?" he asked Ladigo.

"I know nothing about them. In fact, I have never touched one. Knives I have used for many years."

Zeke nodded. "I suspected as much. Well, I reckon as how you'll have to learn a whole lot about using a gun in a short time. I suppose you're going after the judge and his gang tonight?"

"Yes, that is why I am here. The judge is supposed to have property deeds. I will see them."

The old mercantile man shook his head while muttering a few words. "God help you Ladigo. I fear for you, lad." He finished his coffee before dropping the holster and gun belt on to Ladigo's lap. "Put this around your waist. The holster has been greased inside. It will help you make a faster gun draw." Taking the gun from his trousers he inserted five bullets into the six-gun's revolving chamber. "Five only, remember that, Ned. Keep the sixth chamber empty for the gun hammer to rest on unless you want to accidentally shoot your foot. To fire the gun, cock the hammer back all the way like this." Ezekiel did so. "Next, squeeze, don't yank, the trigger. As the bullet is fired, the gun will buck in your hand. And finally, make sure you hit what you're aiming at. Hold the gun in your right hand, aim your right hand and arm at what you want to shoot, and you should hit it." He paused a moment to stare at the young man he was facing. "I feel like I'm sending you to get yourself killed."

Ladigo smiled and shrugged. "You must not think that. What I hope to do is my own doing. If I fail, I fail. Somebody has to stop them. I have to try. I cannot sit by and do nothing.

I am not like Father Jones and his followers."

Ezekiel nodded. "I figured that. Good luck, lad. God be with you."

CHAPTER SEVEN

Ladigo thanked the clouds blanking out the moon and making the chilled night abnormally dark. The darkness he would use to his advantage. He became a lurking shadow that moved silently forward toward the three remaining drunken guards who were noisily shouting.

"Hey, Slimmy, my bottle's empty."

"So drink some water out of that horse trough near you, Buck." Slimmy's laughing answer cut through the night air like a steel cold knife slicing at Buck's thirstiness.

Buck coughed. "Water will rust my stomach. I don't want that kind of iron floating around in my gut. I need something to drink. I need whiskey, lots of it. Come on, Slimmy, you're a whole lot closer to the saloon than I am. Get me whiskey for my parched throat, big bottles, along with some tobacco pouches, papers, and a box of fire sticks."

"All right, Buck. Hold your horses. I'll get them for you, and some for myself. I'm one swallow away from an empty bottle. I've been suffering a whole lot from that long ride we took to get here. All that trail dust clogged my mouth and nose to where I'm still not breathing or spitting the way I should. It's made me a powerful thirsty individual. Ah . . . nuts to everything. Come on, Buck. What do you say to the devil with this watch dog nonsense over the judge and the sheriff? Let's me and you wander on over to that there watering hole saloon for lots of its gut dissolving booze. Their whiskey is guaranteed to galvanize you for two whole days afterwards if you drink enough of it, which I intend to do.

Knuckles can do all the guarding for the city's Mister Important Judge and that snake ornery Sheriff. Hey there, Knuckles, do you need anything, whiskey, smokes, maybe a little sweet-smelling-good-tasting-saloon-honey to keep you warm, huh?" Slimmy called. When Knuckles didn't answer Slimmy laughed and said. "Well now, I reckon as how old Knuckles is more than likely snoozing away. Did you know that ornery-sidewinder-snake could fall asleep standing up? I saw him do that one time when we were both in a Confederate prison and at attention in front of a stupid Sergeant Major listening to his usual rawhide treatment about our being nothing but a lazy bunch of no good Blue-Belly Yankees. For ten whole minutes, Knuckles snored his way through the sergeant's Confederate-type speech. Well, to the blazes with Knuckles. We don't need him to tell us how to get drunk. We know how, and we can sure enough do that on our own."

As for Knuckles, he never felt the two smashing blows Ladigo delivered to the back of his head that put him face down in the dirt.

Except for one light in the hotel, the rest of the building was dark. It squatted, much like a hideous monster ready to pounce on victims that approached it. The judge would be there, waiting, and likely not alone. Ladigo felt the man was a coward who more than likely was liquoring it up in a futile attempt to build courage he would never have. That thought caused him to smile and whisper, "Well, you did tell them you were coming? Don't think about it. Let's go do it. It's onward and upward."

CHAPTER EIGHT

Sheriff Marko was halfway sober and felt his usual snake ornery self. His itchy trigger finger was telling him he needed to finalize somebody . . . anybody. He sneered at the judge, a worthless drunken piece of horse dung finishing a bottle of whiskey, a man who needed killing. Someday . . . someday he would do just that .

The judge downed a fourth glass of whiskey. He burped and slurred words at Marko. "Did you see the way that man stared at me? He got in my skull, saw what I was thinking, that I was afraid. Who was he?"

"He said his name, Judge. Ladigo, Ned Ladigo."

Follett slobbered as he reached for the nearly empty liquor jug. His face telegraphed the fear he was feeling as he mumbled to the sheriff. "The man will come as sure as I'm going to drink a fifth glass of this rot gut burning my insides."

Marko laughed. "I'm ready for him."

Follett shook his head. "I doubt that anybody alive would be ready for Ned Ladigo."

Sheriff Marko laughed a second time.

When Ladigo crashed the door into kindling, the judge screamed once and a smell from his honor permeated the air telling of suddenly soiled undergarments. A startled expression raked the sheriff's face as he reached for his holstered gun.

"Don't, Sheriff. Don't move your right hand another inch,"

Ladigo commanded. "The deed," he yelled at the judge. "Get it!"

"I don't have a land deed." The judge's voice was a croak, similar to that of a crow suffering from a bad cold. Ladigo couldn't help smiling at its sound before he said, "Among that mess on your desk, I see paper and writing pens. Write out a deed giving Father Jones the right to build a church and own the said property the church will rest upon. You will then sign it, making it legal, and Sheriff Marko will sign it as a witness."

In a few minutes it was done. Ladigo grabbed the paper, stuffed it in his right shirt pocket. "Now," he said, "that safe next to you, open it. Take out five thousand dollars and hand it to me. That amount should cover the cost of clearing away the burned rubble from the old church and the building of the new one."

"That's all the money I have," the judge protested.

"Well, you'll just have to learn how to live without it. But be of good cheer. Try to realize the goodness you're about to give Father Jones, who will surely put your money to a proper use. And perhaps he might even thank you for your generous donation. Now get the money."

Judge Follett opened his safe. As he grabbed the money, in the corner of Ladigo's right eye he saw Sheriff Marko's right hand move for his gun in a swift blur. But as quick with a gun as Marko was, he failed to be fast enough. Ladigo's index finger twitched on the weapon's trigger. The gun roared. Its lead bullet smacked Marko's forehead, instantly killing him.

Ladigo stared dumbfounded. He had shot Marko, killed him, something he had never done, nor ever wanted to do to any human. He dropped the gun and kicked it away from him. His felt his stomach churn, rush upward to his teeth, spill from his mouth to land on the floor, and his shirt front.

A man dashed into the room. A gun was in his right hand. Ladigo was slumped near the left wall vomiting and muttering something about an accident. "Didn't mean to kill the sheriff . . . gun went off. I'm a murderer . . . murderer . . . murderer . . ."

Judge Follett shouted. He fumbled for a gun and found one. "I'll shoot you," he yelled at Ladigo. "I'll fill you full of holes. You killed the sheriff, deliberately murdered him." Insanity flashed on his face, maddened his blue eyes. He slobbered sour smelling saliva and shouted, "You killed the sheriff. I'll kill you."

Follett waved the gun around the room squeezing its trigger, firing bullets insanely at Ladigo and the stranger. But the man with the gun shot Follett. The judge's eyes showed a startled look as he fell to the floor next to Sheriff Marko.

CHAPTER NINE

The stranger introduced himself to Ladigo as Jake Larson. Larson sat in his rented room's only chair, his hands resting on the chair's back. As he slowly spoke, his voice lowered. A brotherly expression appeared in his steel grey eyes, along with a single tear.

"Listen to me as I'm talking at you, Ned Ladigo. I've never forgotten the first man I killed. I don't think anybody ever does. With me . . . It was a whole lot of years ago in a one-horse town that a strong wind could blow away. It supported a single filthy saloon. I was trying to cut up and swallow an over-cooked steak and drink a watered-down bottle of flat tasting sarsaparilla. I was seated at a table near the bar. A young waddie that had evidently had too much to drink was showing off about how fast he was with his guns. Six young cowboys crowded around him for the free drinks he was buying. This went on for a while until I found him standing in front of me. He shouted words at me how I was to be his live target. At first, in between chewing and swallowing steak, I laughed at his nonsensical words. My laughter caused him to become viciously angry, to where his left hand shot out to upset my table.

Steak and sarsaparilla splattered the floor as he said, *Draw, you yellow coward, you stinking buzzard.* I had no choice. The kid was fast, good with his guns, but not good enough. A couple minutes later I was puking in an alley, realizing what I had done. It took a long time for me to live with that first killing. You never quite get over the realization of being the person that has killed a human. In time you learn to shove such thoughts as that into the back part of your mind. A few days later you somehow convince yourself the one you killed deserved it." Larson paused to roll a smoke, lit it, and made smoke rings at the ceiling before saying more words. "I live by my guns. Many men I've faced, outdrawn, and robbed them of their future. By reputation I'm a gunslinger for hire, a merciless killer with no emotion, and no friends . . ."

"Ladigo, the judge and the sheriff were as rotten as humans are capable of being. Try to realize that, and also try to imagine what they might have done if they were still alive. Our killing them has helped many people survive, and perhaps some of those people will go on to achieve the greatness they deserve. Think about that as you wallow in self-pity on my bed. Pull yourself together. You've killed a person. Before you're through with life, you'll likely kill more."

Ned Ladigo managed a nod. He smiled, just a little.

CHAPTER TEN

Ezekiel woke up early. He stood, folded his bed blankets, then clothed himself properly for daily work in his store.

Among the ashes in the stove were a few chunks of wood that still glowed with life in them. He added more wood and reached for the coffee pot, which had been left on the stove and was still lukewarm. Should he drink yesterday's coffee? Being a frugal man, he decided its bitter taste would not harm his stomach. Two sips and a grimace later he dumped it.

He heard a soft movement in his shop. Someone was inside.

"Make fresh coffee," came a voice. "I'll light candles. Don't do otherwise. There's a gun on you."

In a few moments Ezekiel saw who owned the voice. Jake Larson smiled and holstered his gun. "Sorry about waking you and the gun. In my profession, precautions are the reason why I'm still alive."

"Then I'm not going to be one of your targets?" Ezekiel asked. There was a lump of relief in his voice.

Larson laughed. "No, not today, anyway. I'm here to give you some money owed you."

"Owed me? I don't understand."

"Did Ned Ladigo pay you for the gun, the holster and bullets, the knife?"

"No, he didn't. I thought I was sending him to his death. I couldn't take his money."

"Ladigo is alive."

"Well, I'm certainly glad to hear that."

"He killed Sheriff Marko. I finalized the judge."

There was a moment of silence with each man lost in their own thoughts. Ezekiel heard the bubbling sound and said, "I think both of us need coffee with a goodly amount of my special stock in it."

The special stock, of course, was high proof booze.

Two coffee pots later the social atmosphere between the two men was somewhat friendlier, particularly when Larson handed Ezekiel large denomination bills. "The extra money is for the twin-double-action thirty-eight caliber revolvers in that glass case."

The merchant man took a long look at the two six guns strapped to Larson's hips before asking, "Why do you need them?"

Jake Larson sipped his coffee. "I don't. Ned Ladigo will need them for his personal protection."

Ezekiel snorted his disgust before saying, "Guns . . . guns . . . guns . . . I want to live long enough to see the day we can walk the streets of a town without a gun on our hips."

Larson smiled. "So do I," he said.

CHAPTER ELEVEN

A building burned to the ground is a horrible sight for human eyes to view. The church had been almost finished. It had been waiting to create history, waiting to absorb into its wood the words said by the humans who would come to worship.

Jake Larson's sigh was long as he said, "Humans' inhumanity to humans . . . will such inhumanity ever cease?"

"Yes, it will. Good people full of hope, with never-ending strength, will end the evil stalking the land," said a voice.

Larson turned and gazed upon the strong features of Father Jones.

"You're one of the men who torched the church." The Father's voice was spoken in a calm manner. His face and eyes depicted no fear. "I assume you're here to end my life. Before that happens, I wish to know your name."

"Larson, Jake Larson."

"You're the famous gunslinger."

"Hardly, Father Jones. I'm Jake Larson, gunslinger. Killer for hire describes me better than the word famous."

"Perhaps. And you are here to . . ."

"Here to give you this." Larson loosened two buttons of his shirt. He pulled out a huge amount of money and a white sheet of paper. He handed it all to Father Jones. "The money is to rebuild the church. The paper is a contract that legally declares you as the owner of the property the church is on. It's signed by the sheriff and the judge."

A minute passed as the Father was at a loss for words. His

jaw moved three times as he counted the money. He finally spoke. "There's close to ten thousand, more than enough . . . I . . . I cannot take any of this . . . you must take it back . . . all of it . . ."

"Why?"

"The sheriff and the judge will not honor the contract. They will come with their weapons and use them."

"No, they will not. The men you fear are dead. Their deputies have fled the city, for parts unknown. You and your people are free. Be happy. Build your church."

"We shall. The sheriff and the judge. How . . .

"It is best for you not to know how they died and by who. Justice was served."

As Larson urged his horse into a gallop he was smiling. His money belt was quite a bit lighter.

CHAPTER TWELVE

With their spurs off their boots and during a moonless night, Larson and Ladigo smuggled themselves out of town. Larson acquired a fast horse already saddled, along with a spare one, thanks to the sympathetic Livery Man and his near to empty money belt.

At the mercantile, Zeke Ezekiel opened his outer door to Larson and Ladigo. He quickly lit only one candle with the hope that no one would notice that his store was open. He smiled from ear to ear as he stacked grub on the counter along with ten boxes of .38 shells for the two wanderers whom he surmised to be on the run. With the sheriff and the judge dead, maybe a brand-new-law-and-order would bring peace to the town. It just might happen.

"The city's telegrapher is busy tapping away night and day asking for a marshal to come to this town and stay for a spell. We expect to hear from one real soon," remarked Ezekiel.

An hour later the certain to be wanted men were in saddles and heading for the high and lonesome territory full of tall trees, boulders, and brush that should shelter them from any search parties. At least they hoped so.

"We're going to be wanted by the law," Larson commented to Ladigo. "Both of us did some killing. That means a marshal or a sheriff with some deputies will arrive and start snooping around. If we're caught by the law, we could end up dancing in the air and wearing hemp neckties. I don't have a hankering to do that."

CHAPTER THIRTEEN

Several weeks were to fly away with the wind before a marshal and two deputies trotted their horses into the town's Livery. After dickering with the shriveled up old timer running the stables, money was exchanged, along with locations of the bathhouse, tonsorial parlor, and a place for good food.

Three hours were to pass before they opened the door of the Sheriff's office. The marshal sat in the swivel chair, planked his spurred boots on the desktop, filled his pipe and struck a match. Two puffs and a smoke ring later, he said, "I could use some coffee."

A fire was stoked up in the small stove and water from jugs stacked in a corner filled the coffee pot. Ready-made ground coffee was generously dumped into the pot to make a strong-tasting brew.

The office door flew open as Marshal Sudowsky was sipping his second cup of coffee and puffing smoke rings with his pipe. In came a nervous little man twitching his way to the sheriff's desk. "Where have you been?" the man asked. It was more of a shout than a question.

Marshal Sudowsky kept his voice calm with an icy overtone that demanded attention. "Go back to the door, open it and close it, behind you. Knock on the door, wait until you hear me say come in. When you hear me say that, come in and pull up a chair to my desk carefully without making a sound. Noisy people disturb me up to where I've been known to shoot them."

The little man did so, then sat. He thanked deputy Jacoby for the cup of coffee placed in his right hand. When he swallowed some, he grimaced and remarked, "Your coffee would dissolve nails."

"We like it that way," commented Sudowsky. "The first pot was even stronger. Who are you, and what's on your mind?"

The little man stopped shivering. He attempted to puff up his chest but gave up. "I'm the Mayor of this town, Mayor Jackson Thorncroft Snodgrass. I'm at your service, sir. I see you have noticed the wanted posters I left on your desktop several days ago. I had them made the day you sent the wire announcing your arrival."

"Yes, the ink seems to be almost wet."

"Well?"

"Well what?"

"What's your answer to the posters? Surely you agree to the amount offered, and the wanted dead or alive section for the murders of Sheriff Marko and Judge Follett."

"Are you sure it was murder?"

"What?"

"You heard me. How do you know it was murder? Did you see Ladigo and Larson shoot the judge and sheriff?"

The mayor huffed wind for several seconds before he managed to say, "Well no, I wasn't there. But I heard . . ."

"You heard. I heard the world was flat, but it isn't."

Deputy Jacoby was all smiles as he poured coffee into Sudowsky's empty cup.

The marshal sipped, stopped to fill his pipe, lit it, and finally said to the mayor. "Get out of here. Leave, before I decide you should be jailed for false information and disturbing my rest period."

Snodgrass huffed. His mouth opened to say more. His jaw

moved, he swallowed twice. His face reflected defeat. He turned and faced the door.

"Close the door softly as you leave, or I might shoot you," the marshal declared.

The mayor left. Sudowsky took a better look at Ladigo and Larson's wanted poster. A feeling came to him, one that through the years had never failed him. "This poster isn't right," he said aloud.

Deputy Thompson came to him. "What's up?" he asked.

"I'm not sure." He stood. "I'm going to ask the townspeople about Ladigo and Larson. If I don't get the information I want, I'll go looking for those two. I could be gone a short time or a long time. In the meantime, you two are the law."

Chapter Fourteen

Slinky Davis and Kirk McGraw gulped the bar's rot-gut whiskey. Slinky was short, chubby and had only one thought in his bulbous head, keeping his knife sharp so humans could be butchered easily. Their table had two chairs. Slinky slumped in one, McGraw, tall and beanpole skinny, sat in the other fiddling with his gun.

A bottle rested on the table. It was half full.

Slinky's glass was empty, McGraw's glass was to his mouth and being emptied. Both men were drunk.

Slinky threw his whetstone and knife on the table. He grinned, showing a near toothless mouth as he grabbed the knife and applied it to the whetstone.

The slithering sound of the knife being sharpened sent chills up McGraw's curved spine. "Slinky, do you have to do that now?"

"Yep. There's a little spot of blood still on the blade. I wonder who it's from, the father, his wife, or the young daughter. The daughter was most fun of all. She screamed loud enough to shake the house's rafters when I started cutting on her." He sighed, "She died way too quick to suit me. McGraw, did you have to gun the father and mother? My knife wanted them alive and screaming as it slowly cut them up."

McGraw emptied his glass and poured it full from the bottle. In one gulp he downed it. "Your knife isn't alive, Slinky. It's nothing but a hunk of steel attached to a human bone handle."

"My knife is too alive, McGraw. You know it is. Why, it

keeps talking to me, telling me it wants more and more cutting on people. It's always hungry for more blood."

"All right, all right, let's change the subject. Look who just swung through the doors."

Slinky looked "Hey, that guy's wearing a badge. Who's the sidewinder with him?"

"I don't know. But I aim to find out." McGraw stood and checked his gun.

"Hurry and do it, McGraw. My knife wants him."

"Slinky, shut your face and listen to me. I'm going to the bar and order a beer. I'll stand close to the lawman so I can hear what is said. Give me money for the beer."

Slinky handed McGraw a dollar. He waited patiently for his partner by filling his gut with what remained in the bottle.

McGraw returned. "Get off your ass, Slinky. You and your knife are going to have some fun. We're going to kill that badge wearer."

After McGraw shot Ezekiel in the stomach, McGraw made him talk. Lawman Sudowsky was going to locate Ladigo and Larson by taking the fastest route to them.

For a few seconds Slinky used his whetstone to make sure his knife was super sharp. He stripped clothes from Ezekiel's body. His knife wanted only skin and bone. Clothing would dull its keenness.

Slinky laughed as he joyously did things to Ezekiel's body. Later, what was left did not resemble the merchant man.

The livery man was next. He received a bullet in the forehead. Slinky giggled and used his knife.

Father Jones was up high on a ladder. He was ready to pound a final nail to a board that named the church and welcomed everybody.

McGraw's bullet crashed the father to the ground. Slinky moved forward, knife in hand, ready to enjoy the butchering.

"Don't touch the Father," McGraw commanded. "Slinky, leave him alone."

"Why?"

"Because I said so. You and your knife have had enough fun. Leave the Father alone."

"But my knife is still thirsty."

"It'll get a good drink on the badge wearer. Come on, let's get out of here before this bunch of do-gooders decide to take action against us."

CHAPTER FIFTEEN

"Ladigo, you've become an excellent shot, thanks to several weeks of my training," Larson said. They rested close to a small campfire, sipping lazily on their second cups of coffee. In spite of their daily noisemaking due to practicing gun fire, they were both quite certain that their seclusion meant no one would find them.

The voice came from the night's cloudy darkness. "Your coffee mixed with chicory smells nice like. I could certainly use a cup or two. Mind if I join you?"

Ladigo reached for his guns, but Larson's whispered words stopped him. "Don't make a foolish move that'll get us killed. Keep those thirty-eights holstered. Whoever is out there has us covered."

"Yeah, you're right. You certainly picked a fine time to have your guns stashed away in your saddle bags."

Larson chuckled. "Remind me to always wear them from now on. Who would have thought I'd need them way out here?"

"It was all that shooting noise I've been making for weeks. It was heard."

"Likely."

"You're still better with a gun than I am."

"I sorta figured I always would be."

The voice came again. "I ran out of coffee and cigarette makings two days ago. I could use both."

"Are you alone?" Larson asked.

"Yep. Just me and my horse. Old Drover is happily

chomping away on some long grass I'm hiding in. Just in case you're so inclined to send a bullet or two in my direction."

"My partner did reach for his guns until I told him not to. I sort of figured there might be more than one of you hiding away in the dark, drawing beads on us and getting ready to fill us full of holes if we tried for a shootout. Well, if you're really just a coffee thirsty hombre who's also in need of a good smoke, and you're all alone, then come on in. Bring your cup and your pipe with you. The coffee is hot, the chicory is turning it black, and we can also spare you some tobacco," Larson said.

The first thing Ladigo noticed about the big man who stepped into the light of the campfire was the badge pinned to his plain white shirt.

Ladigo almost chuckled. "Nice going, Larson," he said. "Well, you invited the law, so you pour the coffee and offer him some of your tobacco." He gazed at the man, "I'm Ned Ladigo. The guy without his guns is the feared-by-everybody gunslinger, Jake Larson. Your handle is . . ."

"Marshal Ryan Sudowsky. I've been trailing you boys for weeks, which is why I ran out of coffee and tobacco. Wanted to ask you why you gunned down the sheriff and the judge. Saw your wanted dead or alive posters, real fancy ones and not to my liking, which is why I decided to track you down to hear your side of the story."

It took a while. The campfire blazed with additional wood thrown on it, the coffee pot was refilled, tobacco was smoked, and what actually happened to the sheriff and the judge was told, first by Larson, and then by Ladigo.

The marshal nodded his head in agreement several times. His last nod came a second before Hell exploded with gunfire.

There was no time to think. Ladigo's hands blurred downward toward twin revolvers. He fired them again and again until they clicked on empty shells. Silence came, for just a few seconds. One of the ambushers was still alive with several bullet holes in his chest. He croaked out a sickly laughter. "We did it, McGraw . . . We got the marshal . . ."

McGraw was dead from a bullet between his eyes. The other man's face shed tears as he dropped to the dirt next to his partner. He took one last breath before death claimed him. His left hand gripped his knife. The whetstone was in his right.

Ladigo hadn't been shot, nor had Larson. Marshal Sudowsky was unconscious, down and bleeding from a bullet wound in his left shoulder.

Larson's face expressed his surprise. "You just killed two men," he said. "Any regrets?"

"No. None at all, thanks to your training," Ladigo answered. "What's next?"

"Next, we keep the marshal alive."

Larson unfolded a thin bladed jack knife and shoved its blade into the fire. "Keep the fire going, real hot," he said. "The bullet in Sudowsky's shoulder has to come out. If it remains in him, infection will kill him in a few days and we'll have a dead marshal to bury, along with those two mangy sidewinders you finalized."

An hour later Larson tossed the lead bullet from the marshal's shoulder into the fire and washed blood from his hands.

Sudowsky was semi-conscious. He turned his head to gaze briefly at his bandaged shoulder. "Why?" he asked.

After thinking for a moment, Larson shrugged and said. "I don't know for certain. You trudged into our camp without your guns. It doesn't sit well with me to see an unarmed man shot down without a chance to shoot back."

Sudowsky smiled. "That's a good reason," he said as he lapsed into unconsciousness.

The battle against death wasn't finished. A day later the marshal was moaning. and burning hot with fever. With cold water lugged from the nearby creek, they swabbed the marshal's feverish body and listened to the man rage about the law and the lady he loved.

Ladigo was busy burying McGraw and his partner. The soil was hard. The shovel was short handled and dull. His grumbling language became unprintable as the smell of McGraw and Slinky's rotting flesh caused him to gag numerous times. But hours of sweat and toil later, with blisters forming on both hands, his burial duty was done. Swearing one last time, he cleaned the shovel to a shine, stored it away in a backpack, washed his soiled clothes in a deep part of the creek, and bathed himself until he felt clean. As the hot sun dried his body, he began to itch. Why? Was there something in the water?

From the packhorse he donned fresh clothing before joining Larson. While scratching his shoulders he asked, "Has the creek water caused the marshal to itch?"

"No, it hasn't," Larson replied. "Why?"

CHAPTER SIXTEEN

Running Deer was new to the Spirit World. She was angry. Why, when the Spirit World had everything an Indian who is no longer alive could want? The Spirit World had no size. It was infinite, a universe. It had everlasting peace in that all the tribes acted as one complete village of total agreement. Horses were everywhere, as many as you could count. Game was plentiful, and eaten. No one was ever hungry. Daily the huge feast fires glowed. Herds of buffalo and deer roamed the land. In the Spirit World, everyone was happy.

Well, almost. When Running Deer and Ned Ladigo were together, she was always happy. Never even once did she ever show she could have even so much as a mild temper. But now she showed she could become over the top angry and fiercely unhappy.

"I am without my husband," she yelled loud enough to cause the Spirit Universe to echo her sentence.

Running Deer's father shouted back at his daughter with his own angry words for others to hear. Running Deer's mother smiled and said nothing. But not so with Running Deer's father. He shouted.

"We have talked of this before. I still find it beyond belief that you, my favorite daughter, disgraced all of us by marrying a white man."

"I am your only daughter," declared Running Deer.

Her father's face purpled. "Never mind, you still remain my favorite in spite of your thoughtlessness. Try to remember what the white man did to our people. He gave us diseased blankets that not only infected us, but wiped out whole villages. Soldiers would come to our villages to murder men, women, and children. When I attempted to hide, I was found. A soldier stabbed me in my heart with his sword. I heard him laughing as I journeyed to the Spirit World. Our buffalo herds were slaughtered by the white man."

"I love my Ned Ladigo."

"He is a white man! Such love is impossible. You are new to the Spirit World. Soon you will see that you no longer feel love for this white man, this Ned Ladigo."

"You are wrong, my father. I will love him forever."

"Are you so certain? Remember that the Spirit World does not accept a white man. You are lost to Ned Ladigo. You must forget him."

Running Deer fumed for a few seconds, then said, "He was raised by the Naneskos for seventeen summers. In his heart he is an Indian. The Spirit World will accept him when he crosses over."

Running Deer's father stomped angrily away from his daughter whom he loved dearly, in spite of her unforgivable mistake. Something had to be done. But what? That was the question. What could be done? Obviously, no harm should come to his daughter. She was loved by everyone, way too much for a tragedy to befall her. Ahh, but what about that terrible white man? Hmmm . . . yes . . . maybe . . . perhaps . . . why not . . .

"You're sure your casting potions never fail?" Running Deer's father asked of the man he stared at.

Was it a man? It resembled more a hunk of ancient old leather with blazing dark eyes and hands that wandered aimlessly. It also spoke with a gravelly voice, like that of the bullfrog.

"I have forever been a shaman. My magic never fails."

The old buzzard is so old he can't walk without a strong wooden stick. He's not able see beyond his own hand. I should have gone to another Shaman. But this withered up hunk of old crow bait was the closest magic man, and he's also happens to be the foremost authority over all the other shamans.

"Then you can do something to the white man Running Deer loves, this Ned Ladigo?"

The shaman smiled. "Why would you doubt my abilities? Yes, I can. And I shall."

"Then I will give you three of my swiftest and most favorite horses the next time the sun rises," said Running Deer's father.

The magic man chanted as he grabbed the nearest two bottles of his magic powder. He waved his arms in a mystic circle. A puff of smoke later he was joined by a nondescript individual, one who could step into a crowd of people and not be recognized, even by his life-long brother.

"I'm sending you to the white man's world. You must find this Ned Ladigo. You must also stay away from your habit."

"I haven't touched a single drop since I've been here, not even a sniff," said the nondescript man.

"That is because the Spirit World does not have any of your habitual habit. Go now."

"Wait! What shall I tell this Ned Ladigo?"

"Anything that convinces the white man that his love for Running Deer is over, that he no longer has any feelings for her."

"That's a tall order, one that certainly calls for a drink," the man smiled as he faded away.

The shaman sighed and swore. It was too late to call the man back. Just what kind of damage could a drunk do?

CHAPTER SEVENTEEN

Sudowsky's fever broke. Twelve days of complete rest had passed before he felt strong enough to mount his horse. He gazed at gunslinger Larson. No words of thanks were said about how the killer had saved his life. Such words among such men were not necessary. Instead he commented, "We're due in town. Let's ride."

Four weeks later in the marshal's office, the three faced deputies Thompson, and Jacoby. Lawman Sudowsky sat in his desk chair smoking his pipe. He did the talking.

"We stopped at Father Jones' church for several days of rest and talk. The two men who murdered him are dead and buried. They also tried to finalize me and failed. Both of them were killed during their gun battle with Ned Ladigo here. I don't doubt those two killed mercantile Ezekiel and the livery man."

While pouring more coffee, deputy Jacoby said, "A stranger calling himself Milton York, he's the friendly sort of hombre who took over the mercantile. He's doing a nice job running it. As for the livery, Jackson Barnes, a relative of the livery man, has taken it over."

Marshal Sudowsky knocked out his pipe. He looked at Thompson and Jacoby and smiled before saying, "Round up your things. It's time we moved on."

"Wait a minute," Ladigo protested. "You can't leave this town without any law."

Sudowsky nodded. He grabbed Larson's and Ladigo's wanted posters, laughing as he tore them into small pieces.

Tossing them in a garbage can he said, "There's law in this town." He opened a desk drawer and tossed two badges at the guys. "Ladigo, you're the sheriff. Larson, you're his deputy. The law couldn't ask for better men."

As the marshal and his two deputies left to journey wherever needed, Ladigo's mysterious itch ceased. *Now if the chanting that started with the itch would just stop.* It did, a few seconds later. Ladigo smiled as he assumed the role of being the town's sheriff.

Aside from gun barreling a few skulls of hardcase drinkers that kept the jail cells occupied, the town was peaceful. Too much so, which was why one day, Jake Larson dropped his deputy badge on Ned's desk with the following words, "I quit."

Ladigo forced a grin. He had expected Larson's uncertainness about being a deputy, a genuine man of the law. "Mind telling me why?" he asked, although he already knew why.

Anger etched Larson's face. "Dammit, Ladigo, listen to what I'm going to say. I'm a gunslinger, a killer for hire. You name it and I'll do it, for the right price. On my eleventh birthday I was forced to start robbing for food. I became an outlaw. It was me against the whole wide world. I'm not really working for the law, I'm hiding behind it. Well, I can't hide any longer. I quit."

Ladigo nodded. "All right, even though I understand your way of thinking, it's all cockeyed crazy. You're a great deputy and I need one. I need you."

"The mercantile man can take my place."

"Nonsense, Jake. Milton York couldn't hit the side of a barn with a gun, even if he was standing inside the barn."

"You're dead wrong, Ned. Milton York is a fast draw, a dead shot hombre, who can drive nails into posts."

It took several seconds for realization to stab its way past Ned's curly hair. "So you're the reason for all the gunfire sounds coming from the shooting range. I suppose York has agreed to become my deputy?"

"He has."

Ladigo smiled and nodded his head. "I suppose you had this planned for a spell?"

"I have."

"I'll miss your being my deputy, Jake."

"You won't."

A few months passed before the itch returned along with the chants. Ned steeled himself and attempted a joke. *Well, and where have you been? Haunting somebody else, I presume?* Days of trying to live with it became sheer hours of torture. There had to be a way to stop it, before he ended up a nutcase. Store bought salves from the mercantile, guaranteed to help or your money back, gave him no relief.

The day he returned to the town and became the sheriff for a time, the itch and voices had stopped. Was that an answer? That the itch and those intolerable ancient chants would stop? If he left the town, found some other place? Became a lawman? There was only one way to find out. He handed the sheriff's badge to Milton York and rode out.

He wandered, just him and his horse, looking and hoping for the itch and chants to stop. They did, a week later in a shabby town that needed a deputy to patrol its one rowdy saloon.

One night he ended up being elbow to elbow with an individual who, after gazing at his shiny new badge pinned to a blazing white shirt, slobbered, "Well hello there, Ned Ladigo. I've been looking for you, everywhere, in every saloon from here to Mexico. Ned, my boy, how are you? I'm Ira Bates, and I know everything there is to know about everything. Tonight I am also a man of the cloth."

Bates spilled whiskey into his gut as he was being steered to a corner table. "I have long searched for you, Ned Ladigo," he mumbled. "Ask away and you shall receive answers." He breathed sourly into the lawman's face.

"If you truly know everything about everything, then tell me why I began itching and hearing chants for some time now."

After two more whiskey shots guzzled quickly by the man, he said, "time to me is not a relevant item. I possess the ability to declare things before they happen, or after they happen. I prefer the after, which means you started to itch and hearing chants before I caused them, or did Running Deer cause them? She is still very much in love with you, while her father adamantly disapproves of you. Hmmm? The Supreme Shaman of the Spirit Universe does not know the true power he has in his endless amount of medicine bottles. If he knew, I shudder to think what he could do to the Spirit Universe."

Before Ladigo could further ask about the itch and the chants, the man who knew everything passed out.

The next day Ladigo had breakfast in the town's eatery. Afterwards he wandered to the saloon and enquired about the drunken bible thumper, Ira Bates.

The grimy bar man sneered and said, "Thank heavens that drunken bum is gone. I hope forever. He rode out of town early this morning on an old swayback horse while owing the bar a whole lot of dollars."

"So where did he go?"

The bartender sneered a second time. "Who knows?" he said, "The way he drinks and brags, there's more than likely a place for him down below."

Did he really know ahead of time about Ladigo's itch and those garbled voices? Ned Ladigo never saw him again. Was the bible thumper a real person, or was he a spirit who was sent to give Ladigo a message but ended up becoming a fall-ing down drunk?

CHAPTER EIGHTEEN

On a Tuesday morning, when darkness still blanketed the town, the itch returned along with the ancient chant. They startled him to full wakefulness as he felt the searing itch racking his body. He screamed in agony and frustration. Damn the itch, damn the chanting. He shouted a string of blasphemous words between grunts and moans and useless scratching, as the chant seemed to say, *Wake up you lazy bum. There are people who need your help. It's time for you to move on.*

With trembling fingers, he lit the candle on the chair next to the head of his bed and grabbed for the pocket watch that was also there. Three hours past midnight. An hour later he was still wide-eyed awake and knew he would remain so through the entire day.

He glanced at his guns, twin .38's hanging motionless on a nail near him, within reach of his right hand . . . a fired bullet tearing out his mouth . . . dying. No, that was not the way to be with her. On a shelf above his desk rested the silver cup engraved with the skull on its front . . . the cup Buffalo Man drank poison from. If he drank from the cup, would he become poisoned? Would he? A single lone dying drink, then a trip to be with her No, that was not the way, either. Were the itch and voices coming from Running Deer? The bible thumper said she still felt love for him.

His body sweated so much his natural stench permeated the office. Sweat intensified the itch and caused him to uselessly scratch.

Meeker was a quiet town with peaceful people,

landowners, mostly farmers, along with a few businesspeople. In this town, the itch and the words coupled with native chants had gone away. But now they were back.

Ladigo snorted a grunt—he'd been almost happy here . . . almost . . . but not quite. How could anyone be happy after losing a forever loved one? Did the itch know that? Did the chants know that? Was that why it had awakened now, to tell him it was time to move on, to look elsewhere, to mount his horse and go anywhere . . . anywhere where the itch and the maddening words might stop short of driving him crazy? If he could just find permanency, perhaps over the next hill . . . maybe . . .or maybe the next trail. Was there a special town or a special situation that offered that? He didn't know. He wanted Running Deer. But in this miserable stinking life he could not have her.

Ladigo groaned one more time before he rose from the cell cot, stretched, rubbed the sleep from sticky eyes, yawned. He proceeded to light more candles and stoke up the fire in the jail's stove. Coffee. He needed strong chicory black coffee.

Two hours later, after consuming a full pot of coffee and a meager breakfast of two fried eggs, Ladigo struck a match and lit a fourth cigarette-sized cigar. With his right hand he ripped the sheriff's badge from his dirty shirt and tossed it at the wooden desk. He shouted orders to his sleepy-eyed deputy that he was now in charge.

Slamming open the front door, Ladigo stepped outside without saying goodbye. After trudging to the stable, he paid what he owed to the livery man and had his horse saddled. Then he mounted Trusty, trotted him to the towns' mercantile, and loaded the horse up with grub for the trail, beans, bacon, coffee, flour, buffalo jerky, two canteens of water, tobacco, and three packs of bullets. His inner voice along with the itch harangued him to forget the town's people, the pretty dance hall girls, the town itself, everything, as he rode off.

CHAPTER NINETEEN

Several weeks of trail blazing did nothing for him outside of developing a sore backside along with thoughts he didn't want or need. Why was he wandering? What was he looking for besides being forever free from the itch and the chants? Would he ever have total peace? Was he supposed to find it? *Help me, Running Deer. Help me find what never ceases to elude me, help me . . .*

With the strength of his will he managed to stop most of the chants and scratch less. And each night, when wrapped into a warm blanket next to a slow burning fire, he would gaze at the seeming closeness of the stars until sleep closed his eyes. He would marvel at their beauty and always ask them the same question. "Why did I fail to prevent Running Deer's murder?"

The stars never answered.

Running Deer, it is so lonely living a life without you by my side.

In his mind's eye he saw himself laughing and crying with her . . . holding her hands . . . feeling the softness and warmth of her touch . . . tasting the sweetness of her lips . . . loving the long walks during quiet nights when the forest animals slept in the silent woods . . . sitting in their secret place with their backs resting against their favorite tree . . . savoring the warm summers with her . . . the thrill that coursed through him in the early dawn as he reached out to softly touch her . . . to feel her warmth . . . to hear her soft breathing as she slept . . .

He was up at the crack of dawn, in the saddle, fighting the

silent emptiness of his ride. Thoughts he couldn't stop came to him. *Life, what was it? To start with, you were born. As you matured to manhood, you realized people were dying around you, your mother, father, relatives, friends, Running Deer.* "Is that what life is all about?" he said aloud. "To be born, to watch people die, and then you die? Or is life and death nothing but an illusion? Or perhaps it's nothing but the next gun facing you, just seconds before death claims you"

Around noon, after chewing and swallowing the last of the buffalo jerky without water, he realized that he was in bad need of grub, water, a good shave, a hot soapy bath and something new to wear. His shirt was now ragged and smelled sour from sweat.

Several hours more were to pass before he discovered a trail that was well used by horses and wagons. Minutes more passed before he spotted a small town directly to the north of him.

The sound of gunfire vibrated in the wind. Shouts of people could be heard hollering and screaming. A few minutes passed before he glimpsed cowboys on horses laughing and firing their weapons in every direction.

Ladigo reined in his horse. Should he go around the town, thereby avoiding a stray bullet that might find its way to him, or should he find the town's mercantile store?

A hungry stomach along with the itch and chanting made the decision for him. Seconds later he found himself in the middle of the murderous cowboys and their guns. The town's sheriff and deputies were face down in the street's blood-soaked dirt, among the horse droppings, being stomped into bloody pulps and broken bones by the cowboy's enraged bucking horses. Six liquored up wild-eyed rowdies lurched in their saddles, puking up stinking alcohol over their horse's manes as they emptied their guns at everything in sight. A woman running across the street was shot down. Blood covered her chest area as she fell. Three of the cowboys laughed when they rode their horses over her to shoot more bullets into her blood-soaked body.

Rage soared through Ned Ladigo. He was barely aware of his next actions as his hands blurred downward to cedar-handled six guns. Twin .38s cleared holsters and death flamed from their four-inch barrels. Four of the drunken cowboys were blown from their saddles to land face down in the street's blood-soaked dirt. The other two, rather than face Ladigo's finalizing weapons, turned their horses and galloped off.

Ladigo cursed silently to himself. He should have been here sooner. With his help the sheriff, the deputies, and the woman might still be alive. Damn.

He emptied spent shell cases into the blood drenched street and reloaded. As he holstered his guns the townspeople surrounded him. One shouted congratulations at him, how he had finalized four of the drunken cowboys and wounded another. He nodded his acknowledgement even though he regretted that two had escaped being shot from their saddles. For certain he would have to deal with them sooner or later. Their kind usually came back along with others, most likely fast guns, specializing in hell raising, bullets, and death. Well, he would be ready.

A member of the crowd kneeled and faced the dead sheriff. He rolled the bloody remains onto its back and grabbed at the blood-soaked shirt to tear loose the lawman's badge. He turned and pinned it to Ladigo's shirt. And that was it. Right there in the street he became the new sheriff. A second later the itch and the chanting stopped.

Ladigo nodded his acceptance of becoming the town's lawman and said, "No one is to call me Sheriff Ladigo. My name is Ned. I will stay in this town until I am no longer needed . . . *I will continue looking for answers. Perhaps one or two can be found in this town. If none are here, and the itch and chanting return, I'll look for another trail.*

Ladigo discovered the pleasure of having lunch at the town's most popular eatery, The Steak House. The food was always good and not too expensive.

It was a blistering hot summer day. The restaurant's doors were open in an attempt to clear away the scent of its cooking odors, along with the customers' cigar smoke and unwashed body smells.

Ladigo smiled due to the food satisfaction in his stomach and swallowed the last remaining chunk of a huge steak smothered with fried new potatoes. From his right shirt pocket he removed a silver dollar, spun it for several seconds on the empty steak plate, then picked it up and tossed it on the table's wooden top. Gulping the last remains of a sixth mug of coffee, he strolled from the eatery section of the Dover Queen Saloon. Gazing at the sun filled town's sweltering heat waves, he rubbed the hotness of the tin Sheriff's badge pinned on his left shirt pocket. It silently reminded him that he was responsible to maintain peace and quiet among the town's people and the soon to be coming cowboys from cattle drives, without using his guns, or when necessary using them.

The town's children ganged around him as he walked. He greeted them all with a smile and a handshake as he tousled their uncombed heads of hair. From a small sack hanging from his gun belt he treated them with small peppermint sticks before heading toward his office.

In spite of a hard-set determination not to look, he found his gaze shifting toward the small shop on the town's far corner. It was Raven's Coffee, Dried Apple Pie, and Ice Cream Parlor. The sign atop the building blazed at him. It beckoned hypnotically, a siren's voice, calling for him to come in and visit with Raven.

According to the town's residents, Raven and her mother had opened up the shop a short time before his becoming sheriff and had immediately established a profitable business. Many of the town's people and a few of the nearby farmer families flocked there to gobble up her pie, ice cream and specially made coffee. There was always a line of people waiting to get into the small shop.

Ladigo had accidentally bumped into Raven—at least he tried to convince himself it just happened. It was on a day when a sudden rainstorm had made the streets full of mud-soaked water with no boards to walk on. Raven had hesitated at the swamped street evidently not wanting to muddy up her long violet dress or shiny black shoes. In politeness, Ladigo had touched his hat in acknowledgement of her presence, then he'd picked her up and quickly carried her to safety across the street and to a boardwalk, all the while noticing her beautiful brown eyes staring directly into his grey ones, and how the warmth of her shapely body began doing things to him, creating feelings and thoughts that he had assumed were long dead.

"Ned Ladigo, I knew you would discover this town and me. I'm Raven. Surely you must remember me." She had laughed and squeezed him in a hug his body suddenly longed for. But his mouth held back the scream that wanted to tear his throat to shreds. She resembled Running Deer . . .. Could she be the lovely little lady who had kissed his lips on the day he left the village, ten years ago? No . . . surely not . . . many people could be named Raven . . . couldn't they?

He had carried her to a nearby boardwalk, touched the brim of his hat and quickly walked away.

That night there had been no sleep for him as remembrance slashed him. He had been twenty. Running Deer had seen eighteen summers. Their friendliness had slowly turned into a forever love that would never be forgotten as long as they were blessed with life and even after their bodies were not needed. Now he was alone, so very, very alone, and he had shoved Running Deer into a corner of his memory along with the beginning of traveling the trails, looking for answers and never finding them.

Ladigo convinced himself to stay away from Raven. He must never eat her pie and ice cream nor drink her coffee and never, ever talk to her. She would bring back too many memories, too much pain, the terribleness of Running Deer's death, her dying in his arms, the beginning of his itching, the chant, the wandering of endless trails . . .

He didn't have to stay in this town. Itch or no itch, chant or no chant, he could move on, go somewhere, anywhere, where there was no Raven to tear at his soul, to have him screaming at night, to wake up sweating and weeping. *Find a trail. Lose yourself in the high and lonesome.* Remember your Indian father who said *True freedom can be found only when you're all by yourself among the heat of the desert, or the forest of the trees.*

A wagon train, renegade whites ambushing it, killing his real father and mother, everybody, except him. Friendly Indians arriving and taking the three-year-old to their village. He had lived with them until Running Deer's murder, until there was no more need for him to remain with the tribe.

Crossing the street to his office, Ladigo closed his eyes down to slits for protection against the blazing noon sun. He glimpsed in the distance that a man was riding a dust covered black horse. He reined it up to a stop at the livery stable. He appeared to be stiff, or perhaps badly saddle-sore. He staggered when his boots scraped the dusty street.

Ladigo sighed. Trouble was coming. He knew who it was. The man was not a stranger. At least not a stranger to him.

CHAPTER TWENTY

Those outlaws lucky enough to have never faced Jake Larson's guns had helped spread his reputation by whispering that Larson was crazy, a cold-blooded, heartless, gunslinging killer. Now he was a soulless bounty hunter, a killer that never brought in live bounty. It was a certainty that other things were said about Jake Larson, when he wasn't around to hear them.

The man stood tall, several inches above six feet. When Ladigo rode with him, his frame had packed steel-hard muscle. Now Larson was close to forty years of age with pure silver hair and flashing hard eyes that rarely showed his inner sadness.

From the window in his office, Ladigo saw the bounty killer trudge unhurriedly toward his office door. On the street, most of the fancy dressed street ladies smiled at him in suggestive ways before they wrinkled their noses and shied across the street away from him. He returned their smiles by politely touching the brim of his hat to them.

His hands became busy brushing dust from the ragged clothing his tall, muscular frame wore like a second skin. His black hat was dust covered. It had seen better days, given the two bullet holes it sported. His right hand grabbed the hat from his head and whacked it against his right hip, apparently in a futile attempt at making it acceptable. Tipping it back on his head failed to hide the silver hair curling its way down to meet with several weeks of unshaved whiskers.

As Larson walked into Ladigo's office he received the lawman's nod. The coffee pot was hot and making bubbling noises. Using a second tin cup nearby, Ladigo stood, walked to the stove, grabbed the galvanized pot, filled the cup with the early morning' unfit to drink brew, walked to his desk and placed it within reach of Larson's grimy hands. He then sat in his swivel chair, rammed his feet up on the scarred desktop and waited for Larson to say something.

"Do you still itch and hear chants?" Larson asked. He grabbed a chair, slammed it to the floor at the desk's front, and busied himself sipping coffee. He said nothing else, only stared at Ladigo with a half-smile on his scarred lips.

Silence lasted another full minute before Ladigo said, "I still itch and hear chants. What else would you like to know? Am I supposed to say it's been a few years since I had the pleasure of knowing you?"

Larson gazed with an icy stare at the lawman before he laughed. "Yeah, it has been awhile. I'm surprised to see that you're the law here."

Ladigo nodded. "It happened. Here we sit guzzling coffee, the both of us. We're alive, breathing air, and not hunted by the law. At least I'm not. Are you?"

Larson never replied to that. Instead he chuckled and said, "Do the townspeople know their sheriff was a lawbreaker a few years back?"

"They don't. It's something nobody needs to know. But now that you're here, I reckon they'll soon know."

"Maybe they will. If it suits me. You know, Ned, all the time we rode together you never talked about your past. I know you have your beliefs, or superstitions, or whatever you want to call them, like that silver cup stashed away on the wall above you. I sort of accidentally came across it all packed away in your bedroll. You never once drank from it. It sure must mean something real important to you. And you sure enough became good with those twin smoke poles. I see you still have them."

"It was your skill that taught me how to use them. And I also learned from you how some people needed to be killed. I'm even better now with those old reliable thirty eights. You were handy to have around. You made me into a lightning fast gunman." He sipped coffee and eyed Larson. "Lately I've read in a few newspapers things about you that sort of stick in my craw. They say that Jake Larson has become a killer bounty man who brings in wanted men, never alive, only over the saddle, dead and smelling."

Larson grinned. He sipped coffee, grimaced at its age-old taste before saying, "This coffee is so bad I'm finding it real hard to swallow. I've never tasted worse and I hope it doesn't solidify my gullet. Sure, I'm that all right, a bounty hunter killer who never fails to bring his bounty in over the saddle dead. Murderers, Ned, every last one of them, murderers. You'd have to look hard to find more vicious outlaws who would just up and kill men, women, and children for the pure pleasure of killing. Sure, I brought them in, everyone one of them, over the saddle dead. That way no prison officials would ever be stupid enough to release them so they could commit more terrible crimes." Larson sighed before adding, "If it means anything to you, I've never hunted or shot an innocent person."

"Do you expect me to believe that? I'll look into what you just said to see if that's so. Now why are you in this town?"

Larson doffed his hat, reached into it, and handed over a folded hunk of paper. Ladigo unfolded it and whistled in exclamation before saying, "Well now, a gang of five men led by a woman, with a $5,000 dollar reward on each of them. All are wanted dead or alive. That's a real tall order, Mr. Jake Larson. Surely you're not going after them alone?"

Ladigo flinched when he saw the strange look in Larson's

steel blue eyes. It was a faraway look coupled with intense sadness, for just the flash of a second, to be replaced by their always steely eyed normalness. He'd seen that same look from the bounty killer a few times when they rode the trail together.

Larson asked, "Do you recognize any of them? Have any of them rode through this town?"

"They might have, but I can't say one way or the other. I'm new to this town. Been here only a few weeks. You'll have to ask the townspeople, particularly the beer and whiskey guzzlers that hang out in the saloon."

"I take it that means you're not forcing me to leave town immediately?" Larson almost smiled. "I won't ask how you became the Sheriff. I likely already know. The old sheriff quit, or he was gunned down and you just happened to be on the spot at the right time, which is usually the way such things happen."

Ladigo nodded.

"Nor will I mention a word about your outlaw past," continued Larson.

Ladigo handed the poster back to Larson. He took a tobacco pouch and cigarette papers from his right shirt pocket, rolled the makings, lit it and puffed smoke for a minute before saying, "Ask away your questions to the whole town. Be polite. If you do something not to my liking, I'll come for you. Try the saloon first. Talk to the owner. He might know something to help you."

"Fair enough, Sheriff. I'll be nice to everybody. I could maybe use help with those guns of yours. Care to walk along with me, like old time's sake?"

"Nope. You can do your walking all alone."

Jake Larson finished his coffee and left. Ladigo opened all the doors of the office to be free of the man's stench and his own.

CHAPTER TWENTY-ONE

"If it wasn't for my saloon, The Dover Queen, this town would be populated only by ghosts, dust, and tumble weeds."

Dover Queen loved to brag about his seedy dump of a saloon. The beer was flat, foamless, and watered down. The hard liquor was worse, only consumed by those who desired a short life.

The man himself? Three hundred pounds of sour smelling, unwashed flesh that never felt different clothing than the ones he always wore. Dover was a hulk of filth, a man with one left eye who wore a dirty patch over his missing right eye.

"So why don'tcha drink some of my whiskey? I brewed it myself out of soured potato peelings, a handful of that smokeless gun powder, and pure well water."

Larson smiled. "Maybe later. The poster I showed you. Take a good look. Recognize any of them?"

Dover Queen held back laughter. Sure, he was familiar with them, used to ride with the whole lot a few years ago, until he got tired of always being in the saddle and decided to open a saloon instead. He respected them, and hated them: Zack Morgan, Jeff Daniels, Axel Davis, Matt Carston, Victor Boswell, and their woman leader, Texas Joanne Sanders. Bank robbers, stage robbers, train wreckers, ambushers, murderers, every one of them. Whenever they struck, guns blazed death until there was no one left alive.

But Queen nodded at Larson and pretended he didn't. "They came in to drink my whiskey, say about six, maybe seven weeks ago. A quiet bunch, sat at a darkened corner table, and talked in whispers. Try as I might to hear what they were saying I couldn't, and there's nothing wrong with my hearing."

Larson left. Dover Queen sweated. When talking to Jake Larson he had acted like Larson, bounty killer, bring them in dead over the saddle, was a stranger. Yeah, he was a stranger, all right, but one he knew a lot about. Jake Larson was dangerous, a threat to outlaw life. He had to be stopped. Now!

He smiled as his gaze fell upon José, who was lounging at the bar. For three shots of whiskey, José would journey to Texas Joanne's lair with the message that bounty killer Jake Larson was dead.

Three men sat at a table playing cards. For enough money, those seedy bums could be hired to kill. Dover walked to their table.

CHAPTER TWENTY-TWO

The day was fading as Ladigo started his usual routine of checking the town for its calmness. This time he was being extra cautious. Jake Larson was in town, and Larson was the kind of individual who could stir up trouble in a peaceable church. So Ladigo anticipated trouble, and he got it. When he stepped into the bath house, all hell was breaking loose.

"Keep his head out of water. We're trying to save his life, not drown him," yelled a cowboy.

"Hey, I just saw his eyes open," replied another cowboy. Was Ladigo seeing double or seeing twins?

Before he could ask questions, Larson began mumbling, "What the . . . what happened? I was shoved into an alley. Men began beating on me . . . using their fists . . . hitting my gut . . . again and again . . .I fell . . . stomped my ribs with their boots . . . It hurt . . . I fought back . . .got to my feet . . . fell down again . . . couldn't get up . . . tried to kill me . . . Shouting . . . gunfire . . . surrounded by water . . . trying to help me . . . or drown me?"

Ladigo looked at the men working to save Larson. "There are three dead men in the alley next door. Who's responsible for that?" he asked.

One of the twins smiled at Ladigo. "We are," he said. "Three of Dover Queen's gun-slinging-thugs were busy trying to make hash out of this Larson fellow here. He's the one in the tub, and then they decided to draw on us. That turned out to be a fatal mistake for them."

"Now that you're close to being fully awake," a twin said,

as he dumped more water on Larson's head and shoulders, "you might tell us why Dover Queen would want to make you into nothing but a limp side of beef."

Ladigo heard Larson's voice. "Dover Queen lied to me about my poster. He knows the people, all of them."

"You can't know that for certain," Ladigo said.

"Yes, I can," Larson replied. "As I asked questions, I studied the man's face, the way it twitched, the look his eyes had, the slight tremble on his lips that he couldn't control. Queen lied. He knows them. He knows a lot about them."

"All right, so he knows them. So what does that prove, Jake?"

"Just this, Ladigo, it proves that others in this town should know something about the people decorating my poster, and I need to ask them."

"Not for a while," Ladigo stated. "You're in no condition to do anything except soak up more water." He gazed at the twins. "And just who are you two? What are your handles?"

One twin smiled before saying, "I'm Pete. The rowdy scrubbing away on Larson's back is my ugly twin, Repeat. We we're born from the same mother ten minutes apart. I was the first born. Repeat was the second born, that's why he's not as handsome as me."

Ladigo smiled. Both Pete and Repeat were no more than twenty summers old, with blond curly hair, piercing blue eyes, six feet or more in height, clean shaven, muscularly well proportioned, and deadeye handsome. Women would never fail to notice them.

"So what made you decide to rescue Jake Larson?" he asked.

"You can thank Repeat's lady friend for that," Pete said. "Mavis saw Dover talking to those three human polecats while they were playing cards. They were to follow Larson and give him some permanent damage, like maybe killing him, or if they felt real nice like, possibly just enough pounding on him to where he'd only end up with broken legs and broken arms, kicked in ribs along with severe head damage, and a few other things, to where he would give up looking for that gang on the wanted poster inside his hat."

"Not even killing me would stop me from finding them," Larson muttered. "Now stop with the pouring water on me. Give me a big towel to dry myself. Where are my clothes?"

Repeat chuckled for a few seconds before saying, "If you're referring to that set of rags you were wearing, I burned them along with those things that used to be socks. The boots had seen better days, holes in their big toe area and they also needed to have new soles tacked on. I tossed them in the tavern's trash pile. You're close to being the same size as Pete and me so we took the final money from that money belt that was tied around your waist and we bought you a new outfit. Here's a towel. Dry yourself. Put on your new outfit, because we're taking you to the town's only doctor. If he's sober, he'll bandage and tape up your ribs. When that's done, we'll help you walk to the Tonsorial Parlor for a clean shave and a short haircut."

CHAPTER TWENTY-THREE

"I wanted Jake Larson dead!" Texas Joanne Sanders shrieked those words at José, who had informed her that Jake Larson, though beaten within an inch of his life, still lived.

She grabbed the nearest objects and threw them across the room in an attempt to control her anger. She slapped José, gave him three bottles of cheap wine and booted him out the front door.

"Go home. Get out of my sight, before I shoot you," she yelled at the fleeing man.

It took consumption of a whole bottle and half of a second one, in less than an hour, for Texas Joanne to calm down to where she could do some thinking. "According to José, Dover Queen, that filthy hunk of fat, botched the job by sending three of his stupid thugs to finalize Jake Larson. He's still alive. That means when he's well enough to travel he'll come looking for me and my gang. So let him come. The six of us can set up a nice trap for that gunslinging polecat."

Texas Joanne almost smiled. She finished the second bottle, looked for more and found only empties. She hollered, "Axel, get in here. And bring me some whiskey."

The five members of Texas Joanne Sanders' gang were next door in a rundown shack occupied by them and a family of huge rats. They were seated around a square shaped table playing cards. The deck was missing seven cards, filthy, and so clumsily marked that everyone knew what everyone else was holding.

"Axel, get in here. And bring me some whiskey," she repeated.

Axel Davis was a killer, the most dangerous one of the five. He was fearless. But when he heard Texas Joanne's shrieking voice he trembled, as did all the others.

Matt Carston smirked. "Well, go on, Axel. The boss is calling a member of her herd. Be sure to remember the booze, two big bottles."

They laughed, all but Victor Boswell. "I hope you have enough nerve to finish her off. We've all tried to kill her and failed. Axel, if you succeed, you're the boss of the outfit. Remember that as you face her."

Minutes later Axel returned. The look on his face told them he had failed. Texas Joanne Sanders lived.

CHAPTER TWENTY-FOUR

Before Jake Larson limped — using his cane — through the swinging doors of Dover Queen's saloon, he informed Ladigo that he had every intention of filling the man's rancid smelling body full of bullet holes. Ladigo then informed him that such an act would likely give him a home in a jail cell.

However, nobody seemed to know exactly where the man was located. He had indeed vamoosed. It seemed that local gossip had come to Dover Queen telling him that Jake Larson had not been killed, and that fact had made it necessary for him to high tail it out of town and into hiding. But to where? An agreement finally came, after an hour or so with the to-bacco chewing, front porch rocking-chair-homesteaders, as they splattered their corner of the town's main street with to-bacco mouth cuds, that all three of them had actually glimpsed Dover. They saw the rotund saloon keeper waddle quickly from his establishment, mount the nearest horse, sav-agely spur it, and gallop off. So where was he headed? Well, that too, was agreed upon, after some heated palavering and a whole lot more tobacco chewing and spitting. Dover had headed northward into the hills, and more than likely in the direction of Owl Hoot Town. To add to the bad news, the to-bacco spitters told how Swifty Jones was now the head boss at Dover's saloon. That Swifty was nothing but a burly side-winder, as ornery a human as any mother had ever plopped out of herself and into this world. He enjoyed brutalizing the saloon ladies and was certainly long overdue for needing to be killed. But no one dared face his twin ivory handled .45s that he was lightning fast with. As he was never without them, a few saloon customers jokingly swore how he slept with them still wrapped around his waist. No man knew that for certain, but it was assumed, by the front porch authorities, that more than a few saloon gals would know for certain.

Ladigo's one-time-partner remained in town, still walking slowly, still with his cane, while asking a whole lot of questions. The lawman received a desk top full of complaints on paper and in person from the mouths of befuddled busybody females and Sam Jaggers, who was the mercantile owner. Ladigo didn't like Jaggers. The seedy jasper not only charged too much for his goods, he was also a woman chaser. Jaggers babbled away at Ladigo and shook his head in every direction possible while saying, "Sure those poster people came into my store. They were quiet, never said more than six words, bought lots of trail food a person can nibble on while in the saddle and a ton of bullets. Paid me and rode off without so much as a goodbye or a thank you for your help.

"But that man, Jake Larson." Jaggers shook his head while making a sour face. "He looked at everything I own. He spent all of ten minutes complaining about how I had run out of his favorite candy, horehound sticks. Then he stuck his right hand into the free peppermint stick jar, grabbed a half dozen of them and never once thanked me or even said his name, although I knew who he was. Why, sakes alive, everybody in this town and even the nearby farm land's people know that he's that insane killer, gunslinger, bounty hunter, Jake Larson. Anyway, he asked a whole lot of questions about that murderous bunch of outlaws he's after. He got real agitated when I kept saying I didn't know hardly anything about them, only that they came into my mercantile, bought a bunch of food stuff, some dry goods, and a whole lot of bullets, while never saying more than a half dozen words before they up and paid me for their purchase and rode out of town. That was a couple months or so ago. They left without saying so much as a good-bye, or so long or even a thank you for waiting on them. I did see them heading up north."

Sam Jaggers paused to get his wind back from talking so much and repeating himself. After two deep breaths and a shake of his head, he began again, this time jawing about Jake Larson.

"Right now that gun-slinging-killer is over at the pie and ice cream parlor. I see him sauntering over there almost daily. Do you suppose he's taken a shine to Miss Raven? Don't blame him none if he has. She certainly is a beautiful woman you would want to look at more than once."

Why did Ladigo suddenly feel a pang of jealousy? His mind jumped to the undying love he had for Running Deer.

CHAPTER TWENTY-FIVE

Jake Larson smacked his lips over the last fork full of dried apple pie and ice cream. His gaze met Raven's. Both of them smiled.

"I've never tasted better," he said.

Raven laughed and replied, "Thank you. My mother should be thanked also. She should be here soon."

Minutes later the mother, Happy Dancer, arrived. Her gaze met Jake Larson's and he stared and stared. The mother looked like an older version of her daughter. Larson introduced himself and did more staring.

Two days later hell came to the town's main street. Jake Larson finished eating his dessert, touched the brim of his hat to Raven and Happy Dancer, stood, and strolled from their store.

It had been a long time coming but death arrived on horseback. Larson instantly saw that Ladigo was in the street and eyeing up seven overly galvanized cowboys wasting lead in the air as they lurched drunkenly in their saddles. When he sidled up close to the lawman and nudged his right elbow Ladigo gave him a quick sideways glance and mumbled, "What are you doing here?"

Larson bit off a chaw of tobacco and handed the remains to Ladigo. "I sorta figured you might need some help. What are you trying to do, get yourself killed? Where are all the other people to help you?"

"I told them to stay inside. That this was my fight, not

theirs."

Larson snorted. "Fine, that's just dandy. I happen to be a little shy when it comes to figures, but there are seven of them raw-hiding-gunslingers and only one of you."

Seconds passed before Ladigo replied, "I don't see how I need help from anyone."

Larson said, "Before you can blink your right eye you'll end up full of lead, dead and buried right where you stand. What is it with you? Do you want to be killed?"

"Maybe I do. And that's no concern of yours."

"Well, you're not going to be pushing up flowers if I can help it. Count me in. I came here for the reward money on that poster I showed you, and also for a special reason that's none of your affair. I intend that to happen. Those gun slingers giving you the eyeball treatment would sooner or later end up chewing on my lead, no matter what, so it might as well be now. You need a helping hand, my hands, just like our old days. Why am I standing straight with you? I don't know. My guns are here and that means so am I."

Ladigo spat tobacco juice. "You used to be chain lightning with those hunks of iron dangling from your hips. You never missed what you shot at either."

"I'm even better than lightning now. For accuracy, well, I'm able to drive a nail at a distance of thirty paces from where I'm standing six times out of six."

Ladigo nodded. "Reckon you'll do. Care to tell me why you're here rubbing away at my elbow?"

Jake Larson laughed. "I already said I didn't know. Maybe it's save a lawman's day."

The seven liquored up lead slingers stopped their shooting at the air and moved their horses into forming a scattered row while an oversized fat man riding a scrawny horse moved forward to the front of the group.

He roared in a whiskey laden voice at Larson and Ladigo.

"I'm Sam Torino, boss man of the herd bedded down a few miles from this here hick town. I'm looking for the man who gunned my brother and several of my best cowhands."

Ladigo roared back at him. "You're staring at the man. I'm Sheriff Ned Ladigo. I'm the law here. You can see my badge shining real bright like at you unless you happen to be too galvanized with cheap liquor to where your eyes can't focus a sober look."

"Well, well," shouted Torino. He smiled and laughed before turning in the saddle to face his men. "Boys, take a real good look at a live sheriff who's about to become a dead sheriff."

They were all hardcase gunslinging cowhands, liquored up to their teeth. They laughed over Sam Torino's words. The fat man turned back to face Ladigo. Slurring his words he boasted. "You killed my brother, Snake Torino."

Ladigo nodded. "I might have, not really certain that I did. Six of them shot a woman, trampled her with their horses. They needed killing, should have killed all of them. Two of them got away. Think I wounded one, could have been your brother."

Torino nodded and said. "It was. He died on the way here. Fell from his saddle, all swelled up with poison, and crying like a baby. Never took time to bury him. Maybe we should have. He deserved to die. He was a rotten human who started killing when he was a mere tad. We never took to each other, fought all the time. But he was my brother. That means there's a score that needs to be settled."

Sam Torino's face became beet red as he stared at Ladigo. "And you finalized my men just because they happened to be having a little fun. Well unfortunately for you, that makes you a dead man. That is after we're through with you.

"First, mister sheriff, we'll have fun listening to you scream for mercy as we skin you alive and shoot you full of holes.

After that, what's left of you, we'll hang you up to where everybody can see you dangling away with the wind. Then to do things proper like we'll drop a few torches here and there into the town's wood buildings, burn them right down to the ground, to where nothing remains but a pile of ashes cluttered with a whole lot of dead people."

Ladigo spat tobacco juice and nodded. "Maybe so, and then again maybe not. You won't be around to find out."

The fat man backed his horse away to where he ended up behind his gunslinger cowboys. "Cut them down," he shouted.

Guns roared and bucked in muscled hands. Men died and fell from their horses. Ladigo slumped to the ground. Larson fired the last bullets from his six guns.

The fat trail boss walked slowly toward him. His smile was more of a sneer as he said, "Well now, peers like the two of us are the only ones still standing. I can fix that right now to where I'm the only one standing."

Larson heard the clicking sound of a six gun's hammer being pulled back and cocked just before a shotgun blast blew half of the trail bosses head into a bloody pulp. The rest of his body dropped where he stood.

Raven ran from her ice cream parlor shouting, "Quick! Grab Ladigo, Hurry."

Chapter Twenty-six

Ladigo spit out the piece of wood the town's drunken doctor told him to chew on real hard. It was to stave off the pain as the alcoholic physician prodded away in his attempt to remove bullets from his left shoulder and his right leg. Chomping on wood didn't help. The doc's probing of his wounds hurt like branding irons scorching his insides.

"There we go." The doc smiled as he said to Raven's mother, "I just got the last two bullets from Sheriff Ladigo's left shoulder and one from his right leg. It was a waste of my time. He might live a day or two. After that he'll be dead."

"Tell me more, doc," Ladigo managed to groan at him. "Two days, you said?"

"What makes you think such a thing?" asked Happy Dancer. "The sheriff is a strong man. His wounds are not fatal."

The doctor shook his head. Words sighed from his mouth. "No, they aren't fatal. His wounds will heal. But *he* won't. It's just a feeling I have." He paused, took a deep breath, and whooshed out enough booze smell to pickle boiled eggs. "I've practiced medicine for nigh on to half a century, everything from gunshots, to fever, to hundreds of births, and dozens of deaths. No one can do all those years as a doctor without developing an inner sense that doesn't happen to be in any medical book. It's something to be felt. Sheriff Ned Ladigo doesn't want to live."

"You're spewing drunken nonsense which I refuse to believe. What can you say about his shoulder?" Larson asked.

The doctor sighed and burped phlegm. "If I'm wrong, and he decides to live, it will heal, but not to his liking. It'll be stiff, useable only on a daily basis. There will be no more left-handed gun-slinging for him. That's if he decides to live." He wobbled for a second or two in an attempt to stand straight, grabbed his black medical bag and said, "I'll come back in a couple of days, though I don't know why I should even bother." He looked sad.

Raven had walked to the bed to stare at Ladigo.

And he, still somewhat conscious, stared at her.

The doctor patted her shoulder. "It's obvious the many, perhaps romantic, thoughts you have for the sheriff. I'm truly sorry for you."

"I'll have mother make extra strong coffee. Won't you have some with us?" Raven managed to ask.

"Not this time. The coroner needs my help. The doctor eyed Larson. "I saw the bodies in the street just before the coroner began removing them to his establishment. One had his face blown off with what had to have been a shotgun full of buckshot at real close range. I'm assuming you had that weapon."

Larson shook his head of white hair. "Nope, I didn't have the shotgun, and neither did the sheriff." He glanced at Raven. "Someone gave us a helping hand, one we needed. It saved me from taking a trip to elsewhere, and more than likely kept the sheriff from chawing on more lead from that trail boss."

The doctor left.

Silence reigned for several minutes, before Happy Dancer spoke. "The doctor is a foolish man who knows not how to properly heal the sheriff's wounds. I know much about the medicines that will heal him. The mercantile man has them."

Happy Dancer ran the three blocks to the Mercantile Shop. She was quite breathless as she dashed into the store. "I need your leaf medicine," she gasped out.

"Why?" Jaggers questioned.

"They will help heal Sheriff Ned Ladigo. He must have certain ones, and you have them hanging from the store's ceiling."

"For a price, and a favor you shall have them. But first the favor . . ."

Happy Dancer saw the sneer on the mercantile man's face, saw it turn to a wanting desire as his glance traveled her body. Well, she had what he needed. Though the mercantile man's suggestion was repugnant to her, she smiled as he advanced. At the feel of his touch and the stench of his breath she reacted in a way the mercantile man never anticipated

Jake Larson fidgeted. Happy Dancer had been gone too long. He threw away the smoke he'd been attempting to build, stood, and ran.

Crashing through the store's entrance door, he saw Jaggers whimpering, sprawled in a lump on the floor. Big X slices bled from both his cheeks and forehead. Happy Dancer stood over him, her right hand holding a bloody knife. She was laughing. Larson grabbed her and kissed her lips. Happy Dancer responded in the proper manner. She dropped the knife and used her arms to enwrap the bounty killer. She returned his kiss, for all of a minute.

"Help me. I'm bleeding to death."

Larson glanced at Jaggers. "Stop your whimpering. Unfortunately, you'll live. Go bandage yourself." He laughed. "I wonder what lie you'll come up with to tell your wife and kids. You'll end up with a face no woman that enters your store will ever look at more than once."

Happy Dancer grabbed the medicine leaves. Larson carried them.

Back home as she ground the leaves into powder and mixed them with water, she talked about Ned Ladigo. "The tribe found him. He was the only survivor. No arrows were discovered, and that told them the wagon train massacre had been done by white killers. A medallion around his neck named him Ned Ladigo. He stayed with the tribe, married Running Deer, then left when she was murdered."

Larson lifted Ladigo's head high enough that the sheriff coughed and then swallowed some of Happy Dancer's medicine. The rest she rubbed into his bullet wounds.

"He will live and he will dream."

"Dream?"

"Yes, Jake. Of Running Deer, he will dream."

CHAPTER TWENTY-SEVEN

L adigo dreamed, not of the Spirit world, but of the time Running Deer and he used to hide from each other.

"I hear your laughter, Running Deer. Where are you?"

"I am at our favorite forest area, among all the trees, where you cannot find me."

"Remember, the tribe says I am their best scout. I will find you."

Ladigo found Running Deer staring into a small puddle of water. Trying not to make a sound, he sneaked up to her and wrapped his arms around her tiny waist. Running Deer, my Forever Love. Tell me, whatever are you doing?"

"I am looking in the water to see if I am beautiful. You keep saying I am beautiful, so I am looking in the water to see myself. Oh, oh, is that me? Is what I see really me? Or is it a spirit looking at me?"

"No spirit is looking at you, Running Deer. You are seeing you."

"Then I see beauty. I see me."

"You are beautiful, Running Deer. Nothing in this world approaches your loveliness. Now it is my turn to look at myself."

"No, my dearest one, you must not look into the water."

"What, not look? Why must I not look? Am I so ugly I would scare the wolves and make the moon cry?" He looked. "Odd. I see nothing. Running Deer, why do I see nothing? Has my image been taken away by evil spirits? Where am I? I am not in the water. Where am I? Where is my image?"

Running Deer cried tears into the water. "You have not crossed over. That is why you have no image for the water to show you."

"Why does it not? The water has your face. Why doesn't it have

mine? What do you mean when you say I have not crossed over?"

"You have not entered the Spirit World . . . it is not time for you to do so."

"Yes it is. It is time. I am here now. I will join you."

"No, you cannot . . . you are not really all the way here. You are struggling between life and death. You will have life. You must have life."

"Why must I? I don't want life. I don't want to live with the terrible sadness of being all alone without you. I want you, now, not some time later. I must have you now."

"No Ned, you cannot and must not have me now . . . You must not. You must go on. I want you to promise me that you will live out your life."

"I can't promise that. I won't promise that. I won't."

"You must. In the years ahead, you will do many good things that only you can do. In life you are very much needed by the people whose paths you will cross. Promise me that you will live out your life . . . Promise me . . . You must live out your life . . ."

"Live out my life without you? Itch forever? Hear your chants and not be with you. No, I cannot promise that. I can't. I can't stand the loneliness I must be with you. I must hold you in my arms. I must."

"No, you are destined to live a long life. You cannot change destiny. Did you say itch? Do you itch? And you hear chanting? How and why?"

"You're not causing it?"

"Of course I'm not! Why would I do such a thing to you?"

"Then who is?"

Running Deer went silent for a moment.

Ladigo watched as an inner fury reddened her face.

"I'm sure I know who. Go now Ned. I must be alone when I deal with my father."

CHAPTER TWENTY-EIGHT

This time the Spirit World's universe was stormy. Lightning, thunder, winds of cyclone velocity, tilting, yes tilting. All of this was done by a normally happy lady who was now as far from being happy as possible. Running Deer was mad, terrifyingly so, at her father, and even at everything that walked and breathed. Running Deer shouted one final time, turning her father's teepee upside down. That was too much.

"Stop," he said calmly. He didn't dare shout. But what should he say next?

"I won't stop. I will make things worse." Running Deer's eyes closed. She opened her mouth to chant, then sighed. She looked at her father. "How could you do such a thing as to send that drunk, Ira Bates, to talk to my Ned?"

"I didn't send him. The shaman did. I never even asked for Ira Bates. Wherever the white man settles, alcohol also settles, which means Ira Bates could stay drunk forever."

"True. Now, I shall turn your teepee into a white man's merry-go-round."

"No, not that. Stop. Anything but that."

"Very well, Father. There are things you must do immediately."

"You have but to ask and I will grant them."

Running Deer smiled.

Ladigo coughed. He felt his eyes blinking several times before what he saw came into semi-focus. He heard a voice. It

croaked. It was his. "Running Deer . . . Running . . . Deer . . ."
He felt a cold rag touching his forehead and then a soft hand
on his face. He felt the presence of someone in the room, and
he breathed in her smell of wildflowers. Was it Running Deer?
He looked, now with clearer vision. No, it was not Running
Deer.

CHAPTER TWENTY-NINE

A few days and a week passed with no itch or chants. Ladigo admitted to himself he felt better. He was ornerier than a Grizzly Bear with an empty stomach. He decided to take his angry feelings out on Larson, to wipe that smile off the guy's face. The bounty killer was grinning away like a cat eating a bird. He even chuckled some, which was a rarity for him.

"Proud of yourself, aren't you, Sheriff Jake Larson? Better shine up that new badge just a little more. It's near to blinding me now with its brightness."

Larson laughed. He puffed some on his pipe before saying, "It's not the badge I'm smiling about, or my being made sheriff because of your being all laid up for a spell. It's what Happy Dancer did to the mercantile man."

He kept puffing on his pipe until Ladigo shouted, "Hey, are you going to tell me what she did to Jaggers, or aren't you? Don't just sit there, propped up all wooden like on that three-legged stool and grinning from ear to ear. Tell me."

Larson knocked out his pipe and shoved it in a shirt pocket, taking his time while Ladigo chomped like he was a horse fighting its bit, before he said, "Well, you know how that General Merchant fellow likes women. Never does he mind that's he married and has children. Anyway, when Happy Dancer dashed to his store for the medicine to help you get well, the guy tried his charm on her. She knifed him, once on each cheek and once on his forehead—"

"Well, is he dead?" Ladigo interrupted.

"Nope. He's alive and kicking. With all the new knife wounds decorating his face I sorta wonder what lies he'll come up with to explain them. I'll bet his story will be a real whopper." Larson not only smiled, he laughed.

A thought hit Ladigo. One he had to ask. "Are you in love with Happy Dancer?"

Larson didn't answer. It was a personal question. However he did nod.

"Well now, and how does she feel about you?"

Again, Larson never answered.

Sheriff Larson decided he wanted deputies. Yes, he needed deputies — two of them would be enough. That would enable him to spend more time watching Ladigo's recovery. And to enjoy having coffee with Happy Dancer. Perhaps . . .

Dover Queen's saloon had a dark corner cluttered by several tables and a half dozen dilapidated chairs. One table and two chairs were being used by Pete and Repeat.

Larson eyed them before speaking. "Howdy boys," he said.

Quickly Pete declared, "We're innocent, Sheriff, been sitting here all the time, drinking up the last of our money."

Jake Larson laughed. "Well now, after all your pennies are gone into gut rotting booze for your stomach, then what?"

The twins eyed each other. Neither spoke.

"Maybe I have a job for both of you. When saving me, you finalized the three that would have finished me off. That proves you're good with those hog legs strapped to your waist."

Repeat nodded. "We can drive nails at thirty paces."

"Okay. Come to my office. I'll deputize both of you."

CHAPTER THIRTY

Pete and Repeat being deputized by Larson allowed the bounty killer to spend a great deal of time watching over Ladigo. At least that was what he claimed to be doing. He even said so out loud and silently to himself. But that was an effort to half-way-convince that handsome guy whose reflection he saw in that small metal mirror he packed in the right hind pocket of his trousers.

Larson became a spiffed-up dude, always wearing a clean outfit, bathing more often, combing his hair every morning, and frequenting the Tonsorial Parlor for an almost daily shave. Why, you might ask, did he decide to do this? Well, Raven's mother, Happy Dancer, was an exceptional beauty, a woman to look at, and Larson looked at her, a lot, in fact more often than he did at that bedridden snake, ornery Ladigo.

Jake Larson judged Happy Dancer to be his age. She was a fair to middling fantastic cook and quite knowledgeable about Indian medicine, which was why Ladigo was alive and on his way to being well. Although Larson knew it was hard for the ornery so-and-so to admit it, especially to himself.

Happy Dancer also knew how to please a man by kissing him. Real often.

But there was a fly in Jake Larson's ointment, actually six flies. The bounty man was determined to find and bring in the killers listed on the poster he kept in his hat. It was something that burned so star hot in his soul that he had to accomplish that task before he said certain words to Happy Dancer.

As the days dwindled on, Ladigo continued to improve,

but his natural orneriness got downright miserable to put up with. Larson contemplated shooting him. But Ladigo wasn't worth a bullet. Instead, the bounty killer pumped the house's atmosphere blue with smoke from his pipe while drinking several pots of coffee on a daily basis as he listened to Ladigo belly aching.

"Simmer down, Ned," he hollered many times. "This town's sorta on its good behavior for a change. My deputies haven't had to shoot anyone. Using their long- barreled-guns they happily cracked the skulls of the saloon's hardcases. And that caused the rest of the habitual booze hounds to quiet down and be peaceful like."

He continued by saying, "Now I've been hankering to talk about a certain lawman whose name I shall not mention, but his initials happen to be Ned Ladigo. I rode with him for a spell. Back then we were considered to be outlaws, though in a way we weren't. But we were partners, sort of like. I took him for a smart man. He fooled me into thinking that. Yep, he sure did. Well, that was then. Now I realize that the man I rode with has gone and turned in to an ignorant cuss, so dumb he can't even notice that a certain beautiful lady named Raven is head over heels in love with him. Never mind that this individual, according to what Happy Dancer has told me, was married a few years ago. Running Deer is dead, in the past, a memory perhaps never to be forgotten, while the other woman is alive and pining away hoping with all her heart that Mr. Ignorant will notice her and love her. Why she wants that ornery-no-good-cuss, I'll never be able to understand."

Larson grabbed the mirror from his back pocket and shoved it close to Ladigo's face. "Just look at you," he said, "sprawled in that bed, pampering and complaining yourself silly, just like a spoiled child. You're a longways short of being an idiot, but you are dumb. Look around you. Take a good look at Raven and the happiness you can have with her. Why she would want you . . ."

Ladigo said nothing. He stared at his reflection and then at the front door, the one Raven and Happy Dancer had used when they left for their ice cream parlor. He breathed in and out. Was Jake right about Raven, and why did he suddenly feel happy?

CHAPTER THIRTY-ONE

Jake Larson informed Ladigo that he was about to lose a deputy. Love had bloomed branding-iron hot for Repeat and Mavis, and their joining in a marriage could happen any day now. Yep, Deputy Repeat had it all planned out, marriage to Mavis, quit being a lawman, become a rancher, and live happily ever after.

It sounded good, until the very next day. Ladigo was struggling to get out of bed when Larson dashed in, white faced with anger, and with words hard to say.

"Mavis went to Swifty Jones to ask for his permission to release her from being one of his saloon ladies. Swifty took his silver buckle belt to her. He beat her to death, just as Repeat crashed through his office door and emptied a gun on him. After killing Swifty, Repeat took off heading up north, toward Owl Hoot Town. Deputy Pete went after his brother. I'm going to go find both of them. I have to bring Repeat in, let him know that he won't be charged for killing Swifty."

Larson had said those last words without looking at Ladigo.

"Why, it's too early for a reward poster on him," Ladigo stated. "Wait until one is printed. Are you so in need of money that you would bring in the dead body of your own deputy? Jake, I never took you for that kind of man."

Larson shouted at Ladigo. "You've got me wrong, Ned. Look at the evidence. Swifty Jones killed Mavis. His silver buckled belt made bloody gashes all over her. She died hard. I say Repeat finalized Swifty real legal like."

"Yeah, that does sound reasonable."

"And I'll bet you a year's pay the six I'm after are also there."

It takes some hombres a hit in the head to realize that once you were a partner, you were always a partner. Ladigo couldn't let Larson go to Owl Hoot Town alone. He just couldn't.

To Ladigo, it hurt as if he was on fire as he struggled from the spare bed in Raven and Happy Dancer's upstairs home above the ice cream shop. He came close to cursing aloud at the pain shooting through his body. But he didn't. Those were words he never used, but he could sure think them.

He struggled with his clothes, shirt, trousers, socks, and boots, then finally a holstered gun around the right side of his waist. His whole body blazed away at him. Jake Larson had already left, and Happy Dancer was crying as she sat facing away from him. He sneaked past her, quietly opened the back door and silently stepped clumsily down the staircase. Now all he had to do was to get to his horse, saddle it, and go help Jake. He hoped.

CHAPTER THIRTY-TWO

At the edge of a thick forest, Ladigo's right boot snapped a twig. He could see Jake carelessly slumped near a smoldering fire. The bounty killer's face wrinkled into a concerned expression, and his right hand grasped a cedar handled pistol.

Ladigo snapped another twig, this time with his left boot which also caused a jingling sound from the stirrup that he couldn't remove.

Larson crawled slowly to the left and away from the smoldering embers of his campfire. His voice was calm as he said, "I have five bullets in this shooting iron I'm holding. In a few seconds I will squeeze off all of them to where I hear you tromping like an elephant with only three legs. You stand a good chance of being hit."

Ladigo laughed. "I could have shot you an hour ago, Jake. Maybe I should have."

"Get in here, Ladigo. Get in here and I'll make coffee for the both of us."

Ladigo limped forward, grimacing in pain and gritting his teeth.

Larson shook his head in disgust. "You're some kind of a fool wearing a half dead expression. Why are you here?." He sighed. "But never mind telling me. You're here, and that's what's what."

"I'm here to help," Ladigo managed to rasp out during his puffing for air.

"Sure you are. That's written all over your face. It's why you're here. But in your present condition, just how could you help? Sit down before you fall down. Some coffee is already made and it's still hot. Your cup will have an extra stiff shot of my medicinal whiskey in it that'll either brace you up or finish you off."

Ladigo tried to grin when he grasped the tin cup handed him. Sipping the whiskey-laden coffee, he coughed and felt it burn all the way down to his innards. "This should keep me alive and half drunk," he mumbled. Three sips later he added, "I hope."

"Shut up and drink," Larson commented. "I knew you'd come barging in on me. Should have hog tied you to that bed you've been wearing out."

Ladigo tried to smile. "And that's why you settled down here, out in the open with a campfire anyone could see, so I could find you, which you knew I would."

A noise was heard out there in the dark among the trees. Ladigo glanced at Larson. "Nobody followed me," he whispered.

The bounty killer was already standing with his gun cocked in his right hand. "Stay here. I'll find out who's attempting to sneak up on us."

"Stay here," Ladigo grumbled. "In other words, I'm the target for whoever's out there, while you sneak around trying to find out who it might be before I get filled full of lead."

Larson chuckled. "Whoever it is could have already shot the both of us. Shut up and drink your coffee."

Larson disappeared. Ladigo was alone. He started feeling scalp hairs crawling on his neck. Slowly his right hand searched and found his holstered handgun. It felt abnormally heavy, telling him he should have stayed in bed instead of being an ignorant galoot out here, who might at any second become a drygulched piece for vulture pickings. He sighed and coughed.

In the darkness illuminated by the dying campfire, the

captured man's face showed clearly.

"Pete!" exclaimed Ladigo as he holstered his gun.

"Have a seat," Ladigo exclaimed, the relief obvious in his voice. "Larson, pour your deputy a cup of coffee with whiskey in it. He looks a bit nervous. Pete, you have some explaining to do, like why were you sneaking up on us instead of just walking in and chatting with us?"

Pete sat close to the smoldering fire for its remaining heat. His body trembled as he accepted the coffee handed him, sipped it, coughed and sipped again.

"Start explaining why you were hiding in the trees," Ladigo demanded. "You had to know who we were."

"That's just it. I did know," said Pete, looking more courageous. "You and Larson are lawmen. That means you've come to take Repeat back, jail him, and then try him. He'd be sentenced and hanged for the murder of Swifty Jones. I'm not going to let that happen."

"Neither are we."

"What?" Pete stammered.

"You heard right." Larson declared. "Swifty Jones was shot dead by Repeat after Swifty killed Mavis. Ladigo feels that your brother is not guilty of Swifty's death, and I feel the same way. We're here to tell him that."

Pete stopped shaking, finished his coffee and asked for more with whiskey in it.

"So where's that outlaw town?" Larson asked. "I haven't been able to find it among all these trees."

"I know where it's at," Pete remarked. "I've been there, and I saw Repeat getting drunk in the town's saloon."

Silence reigned as the two lawmen stared at Pete. Larson was the first to speak. "Did you try to get him out?"

"Yeah, but I failed. The saloon was full of gunmen. I had to shoot my way clear of the joint. Good thing everybody was falling down drunk and couldn't hit the inside of a barn with their weapons or I'd been full of holes. I made it here and I ran into the two of you."

Pete finished his coffee, handed the cup to Larson and said, "I'm going back. Am I going alone or with company?"

The three made it through the swinging doors of the saloon. One sniff of the sour smelling air informed them that their old enemy Dover Queen was presently tending bar. His shout verified that.

"Hey, the law's here. Gun them down."

Handguns were jerked from holsters.

Lead flew. People not packing iron on their hips ran for cover while case-hardened gunslingers screamed and died. When the silence came and the gun powder began to clear away from the air, Ladigo, Larson, and Pete were the only ones remaining on their feet.

Repeat was slumped against a wall, dead drunk, with six knives stuck in the wall around his head.

"We got here none too soon." Pete shouted. "It looks like Repeat was being used as a target for knife practice." He lifted Repeat to his shoulder. "He'll most likely wish he was dead when he starts sobering up. Right now he needs lots of coffee and a place to vomit." Pete left muttering something about needing air for Repeat. Larson remained in the saloon expecting and knowing what had to happen next. Ladigo hid in a darkened corner out of sight.

At the head of a staircase, a woman screamed. Larson looked up and saw Texas Joanne Sanders. Ladigo noticed she appeared to be Larson's age, but still young looking and quite beautiful. She gracefully walked down the staircase one step at a time and moved within touching distance of Larson's face.

"I wanted you dead," she shrieked. "Why aren't you?"

Hatred blazed in her eyes as her lips twisted into a sneer. Texas Joanne Sanders laughed. She spit in Larson's face and shouted. "You're still the sniveling coward I married years ago, a dirty scum of a nothing human who happens to be fast with those deadly playthings dangling from your hips."

"Those playthings were faster than your gang, Joanne. Right now they're all saying hello to the devil."

"And I suppose I'm next. Well, go on, get it done with. Shoot me. Get it over with. Put a bullet in my heart."

"You lost your heart years ago. No, Joanne, no bullet for you. I'm taking you to jail. You're standing trial for your crimes. I've been after you and your gang of murderers for over two years now. Shooting you would be a too easy way out for you."

Texas Joanne stared at Larson. She smiled. "You're afraid to shoot me. That's it, isn't it?"

Larson nodded. "I've never shot a woman. I don't intend to now. But it's more than that. I remember things. Do you?"

"What? That I was married to you? Yes, I remember. That's why I wanted you dead."

"We're still married. We never divorced. What happened to you, Joanne? Why did you form a gang of murderers? Why did you start killing?"

Texas Joanne reached into her dress and grabbed a Derringer. Pointing it at Larson, she laughed before saying, "It contains a divorce bullet, one that says *goodbye Jake.*"

Ladigo wasn't fast enough to stop what happened. A Derringer bullet slammed Larson's left shoulder. As he dropped to the floor, a six gun at the bar roared and Texas Joanne Sanders slumped, grabbed at her chest and fell next to him.

As she died, Larson touched her hand and held it. He muttered. "I used to love you, Joanne. I think I still do, just a little bit, somewhere in my heart."

Larson's words to his dead wife made Ladigo realize that it was possible to love more than one person. He thought of both Running Deer and Raven.

Though badly wounded, Dover struggled to stand upright behind the bar. A smoking gun slipped from his right hand. He attempted to chuckle as he said, "Her gang hated her, and I did too. Well, I killed her," were the fat man's last words before death took him.

CHAPTER THIRTY-THREE

It was a frantic search before Pete and Repeat found a doctor for Larson's shoulder wound. Obviously, if and when the town's outlaws were shot up, there would be a person around who could patch them up. And the man was sober.

Pete and Repeat discovered a few honest citizens, a blacksmith whose partner was a gunsmith, a small group of farmers, and a dozen people who attended church.

They made a decision. "We're staying in Owl Hoot Town. We're going to be the law."

"All right," Ladigo agreed. "The two of you want to bring law and order to this town, okay. I hope you enjoy lead for breakfast, because lots of it will be sent in your direction. Good luck to the both of you."

Three weeks passed before Larson was able to ride. Ladigo and he saddled up and rode off in the direction of the town they now considered to be home.

Larson prolonged his getting well because he enjoyed Happy Dancer fussing over him.

In his office Ladigo poured coffee into the silver cup. He was scared, trembling, yet determined to find out if the cup would kill him or set him free. He raised it to his mouth and drank. A coffee pot later, he handed the cup to the town's bullet maker. "Melt it down and craft it into thirty-eight caliber bullets, as many as possible."

Out back, away from the saloon, were six wooden posts

with nails protruding from them. If anyone tired of drinking or wanted to show off their skill with weapons, or maybe for dozens of other reasons, lead was wasted at the big nails in the posts. Among certain members of the town, driving the nail had become a betting contest. The person who could drive the nail into a post with his first bullet would become a marksman to be feared as the losers handed him their money.

Ladigo had three bullets made from the silver cup. At forty paces distance, he drove the nails solidly into three posts.

Epilogue

So what else could be said about Ned Ladigo? Well, time healed him to become strong as a bear. He liked the deliciousness of ice cream, apple pie and coffee for his breakfast. He sat on one of the tall stools in front of the counter staring at Raven, who stared back at him. Both were smiling in a certain way that those who are deeply in love are capable of smiling. No words were said between them as they held hands. There didn't have to be.

Naturally they were married. Three children made them into parents, two boys that were Ladigo lookalikes, and a daughter as beautiful as Raven. Ned Ladigo remained the sheriff of the town for thirty years. When he retired, his oldest son, Jack Ladigo, became the sheriff. Jake Larson and Ladigo started the Circle LL Ranch. It became the largest in the area, with a herd of ten thousand cattle. Ladigo's son, Mitch, bossed the Circle LL. Ladigo and Raven's daughter, Michelle, owned six ice cream, coffee, and pie parlors around the county and expected to add more. Ladigo's wife and Jake Larson's wife hosted barn dances twice a year, and everybody came bringing enough food for an army.

Ned Ladigo never forgot his first wife, Running Deer. Alone at night, as he sipped a final cup of Raven's delicious coffee, he looked at the stars and wondered what life would have been like had she lived. His memories of Running Deer were fond and not painful anymore, as he lived happily ever after with his family and friends.

In closing this story, always remember that Love Is

Forever.

ABOUT THE AUTHOR

Wow. So just what can be said about Wayne Greenough? Half alligator, half Tasmanian devil and the rest of him, he's just ornery?

Nah, not really! He's actually one of those nice type nice guys who are just a little bit crazy and just a little bit of a liar. Yeah that's him all over, a little crazy in the sense that dozens of stories tumble around in his hollow head until he writes them. He's a liar in that all of his stories are not true. They're all pure fiction and straight from his addled head.

www.ingramcontent.com/pod-product-compliance
Lightning Source LLC
Chambersburg PA
CBHW070507130626
46555CB00003B/1198